THE HOMESTEAD

THE COWAN FAMILY SAGA – BOOK 3

Russell J. Atwater

Contents

Chapter One
Broad Valley

"Broad Valley," Bruce announced as he stood on a large boulder on the bank of the Canadian River and looked across the grassland littered with groves of towering ponderosa. "One hundred and sixty acres from this rock northwest will be my land. And the quarter section of land to the east of it will belong to Trent after we apply today to the registrar in Salt Flats."

The Cowan family smiled, as did Trent and Pat. The only person missing was Pony Boy. He, along with Lobo and Pup, was with the flock of sheep.

Bruce climbed down from the boulder. "Let me saddle up, and I'll be ready, Trent."

"Trent," Becky said as they walked away from the others, "I'm so glad you filed an application for a homestead."

"Yup," Trent said with a smile. "I feel good about it. I'll finally have a permanent home. It's a good feeling. Of course, I won't get a deed to the land until I live on it for five years and build a house."

"Yeah, it will take a lot of hard work to build the log cabins. I'm just glad you and Daddy don't have to do it alone."

Trent nodded. "I'm surprised that Pat and Wes are staying until we complete both cabins. I expected them to hightail it west as soon as they could."

"Trent, are you ready to ride?" Bruce called from atop one of the four Morgan mares that Pat had bought to pull Trent's wagon down the Canadian River.

"I've got to go, Becky," Trent said as he turned and hurried over to Tex. Out of nowhere, Lobo appeared. Trent glanced down and shook his head. "No, Lobo, you stay with Pony Boy and help him and Pup with the sheep." Trent didn't think the wolf-dog understood all of what he said, but he understood the word no. Lobo dropped his ears and turned and headed back to the flock.

"I swear, Trent, your dog has turned out to be worth his weight in gold with the sheep. And to think I was concerned he might kill the entire flock," Bruce said as they headed down the river, keeping close to the bank. "Why hasn't the valley been settled?" Bruce asked as they turned north and rode away from the river.

Trent pointed to a mounted man watching them from afar. "That's the reason. This is Apache territory. Unless you come down the Canadian River from Wagon Mound, you have to ride through Apache country."

"Are they going to attack us?" Bruce asked.

Trent shook his head. "Maybe, but for now, he's just observing us. It might be different when we return. He might fetch a war party."

"Well, let's hope he doesn't. I certainly don't want to lose my scalp the same day I partition for my homestead claim," Bruce said.

The Apache shadowed them for several miles before he vanished.

"They are the best at blending with the land. You only see an Apache when he wants you to see him," Trent said.

Salt Flats lay to the east of Broad Valley and north of the Canadian River. About five miles out of the valley where the canyons gave way to rolling hills, they hit a trail that headed toward town. Hard riding brought them in sight of the town of Salt Flats a little before noon. Away from the river and Broad Valley, the land turned drier. The grass didn't grow as lush or as tall as it did in the river valley.

Trent had been in Salt Flats many years ago when his father had stopped in the small town to trade. From what he saw of Salt Flats as he and Bruce rode into town, it had grown substantially. He didn't remember so many buildings, and certainly not the hotel and bank. He vaguely remembered his father visiting the Cattleman's Saloon.

Bruce looked down the main street. "It's bigger than I expected.

Trent nodded. "It's grown since I was here," he said as they rode down the street. "There's the registrar's office," he added, pointing to a wooden building next to the sheriff's office.

"Well, let's go and file," Bruce said.

Trent didn't know what to expect since he'd never been inside a registrar's office. He didn't expect so many maps. It had taken him and Bruce a while to locate their homestead plots on a plat map. But finally, they finished the paperwork, paid the filing fee, and walked out, smiling from ear to ear.

Trent pointed to the Cattleman's Saloon. "What do you say about celebrating with a shot of whiskey?"

Bruce slapped his hat against his thigh. "Sounds like a grand idea, Trent."

They untied their horses, walked them across the street, and tied them to the hitching post in front of the saloon. As he finished tying Tex's reins, Trent noticed four ranch hands loitering on the porch of the saloon.

"Where did you sodbusters settle?" one cowboy, a young man with an unruly mop of red hair, called out.

Trent shifted his rifle in the crook of his arm. "Half a day ride southwest of Salt Flats."

"Hell, that's Apache country. I guess we don't have to worry about y'all stringing up barbwire. The Apaches will have your scalps in no time," the man said.

Trent patted his buffalo rifle. "Not if I have anything to say about it. I'm partial to keeping my hair."

The redhead turned to look at his companions. "You hear that, boys? This one thinks a single buffalo rifle will frighten the Apaches."

The three other men laughed. "That's telling him, Red," one of them said.

The redhead turned back to Trent as Trent climbed the steps to the porch.

"It should," Trent said. "Now, if you gentlemen will excuse my friend and me, we need to wet our whistles."

Red stepped in front of Trent. "That's just it, none of us are gentlemen. Now, if you think you can swing that rifle around quicker than I can draw my iron, fly to it."

For the first time in his life, Trent realized he had met an opponent quicker than him. It both humiliated him and angered him. He tensed, on the verge of testing his assumptions, when he felt Bruce's hand on his shoulder.

"Fellows, we don't want any trouble. We just want to get a shot of whiskey. It has been a long ride for us." Bruce stepped around Red. "Come on, Trent. I'm buying," he added.

Trent thought of Becky and swallowed his pride. He followed Bruce past the sneering Red. Neither he nor Bruce spoke as they pushed through the butterfly doors of the bar.

Ranch hands dominated the room. If Trent hadn't known Salt Flat as a cattle town, he did now. The few sodbusters who drank in the saloon kept to a separate section in the back. None drank at the bar.

Bruce, however, walked boldly up to the bar and stared at a tall, ugly-as-homemade-sin bar dog until the man stopped polishing a shot glass with a dirty rag and walked over. He just stood in front of them, not offering a greeting of any kind.

"Whiskey," Bruce said and placed a five-dollar bill on the bar.

Without a nod or any other sign that he had heard, the man pulled a label-less bottle with amber liquid from under the bar.

"Hmm," Trent said. "Cheap whiskey. Pat would approve."

"You want it or not?" the bartender snapped.

"Yes, thank you," Bruce said and smiled.

"Sodbusters," the man mumbled under his breath as he filled the shot glasses. He scooped up the bill and left to make change, as though hoping they wouldn't stay for another round.

"You fellows are treading on thin ice," a chubby, middle-aged man with a cherub face said as he pushed his way between Trent and Bruce.

Trent glanced at the man. "Yup, I already know that it's a cow town."

"Oh, you must have brushed elbows with Red, the welcome committee. Good you didn't brace him. He's killed eight sodbusters I know of in shootouts." The man paused and shrugged. "Can't say how many he's bushwhacked."

"Yup," Trent said. "We met him."

"Why is he so against settlers?" Bruce asked. He lifted his shot glass, made a motion toward Trent, and then threw the contents into the back of his mouth. "Wow, that'll take your breath away," he exclaimed as he shook his head.

"The cattlemen association in these parts wants to graze on government land open to settlers along the Canadian River. Once a settler stakes a homestead claim, they can string up barbwire fences. And there goes the free grazing land," the man said. He held out his hand to Trent. "Joshua Muster."

Trent took the man's hand. "Trent McLeod."

"Bruce Cowan," Bruce said when the man turned to shake his hand.

"Nice to know you, gentlemen. Whereabouts are you homesteading, if I may inquire?"

Bruce answered the question. "East on the Canadian where the river exits the canyons. We found a valley. I call it

Broad Valley. It's got rich soil and huge ponderosa pines suitable for building a log cabin."

Joshua started shaking his head even before Bruce finished. "Fellows, you couldn't have picked a more dangerous place to homestead. That valley is sitting under Apache territory. The cattlemen association furnishes the tribe with beef to keep settlers from those sections of the river."

"Why?" Bruce asked

"They run cattle along the Canadian River. That's the best grazing land in the panhandle of Texas. And when the local cattle baron makes a cattle drive, he follows the river out of Texas and heads north. He moves herds of three thousand cattle or more in his cattle drives. Word is he drives them up to the railhead in Cheyenne."

At the word Cheyenne, Trent tensed. "What's the name of the cattle baron?"

"Cord McGregor. He's on a cattle drive now, up to Cheyenne. You met his enforcer, Red, on the porch when you entered the saloon."

Bruce laid his hand on Trent's shoulder. "Whoa, there. Let's not start something. He ain't even here."

"You fellows know Mister McGregor?"

"Yup, we had a run-in with him on the Santa Fe Trail. He tried to stampede his cattle into our wagon train."

"Yeah, he hates the dickens out of settlers. But running his herd into a wagon train, that's a little far for even Mister McGregor. What did you' all do to provoke him?"

"I'm half Yaqui," Trent said.

"Oh yeah, that'll do it. He dang sure hates Indians more than settlers. It galls him to have to deal with the Apaches to keep the settlers away from the river. However, that's the only legal way he can keep the settlers out. I guess he sees dealing with them as a necessary evil," Joshua said, shaking his head. "But one of these days when he figures he doesn't need them, he will swoop down with his men and massacre the entire tribe."

A cowboy in dusty chaps rose from the nearest table and walked over to the bar. "Why are you sodbusters jawing about Mister McGregor?"

Joshua turned around. "Oh, Leroy, I was just telling my new friends what a dandy neighbor Mister McGregor is."

"You are lucky he hasn't squashed you like the cockroach you are, Joshua."

Trent brought the butt of his rifle up to hit the man below his chin. The cowboy fell backward. He hit the floor with a thud and didn't move.

"I don't take kindly to someone talking to my friends that way," Trent said to the men staring at him in astonishment.

Joshua downed a shot of whiskey and touched the brim of his hat. "Got to go," he said as he rushed for the door.

The sodbuster barely got out of the door when Red rushed inside. He spotted the man on the floor and grabbed for his gun. However, Trent had expected the action and fired his rifle. The big caliber shattered the handle of Red's Colt before he touched it.

Trent lifted his rifle off his shoulder as he drew his pistol. "Don't anyone move."

Silence.

"You've done it now, sodbuster," Red hissed as he looked down at his ruined pistol.

"The name is Trent McLeod. McGregor knows my name. I had a run-in with him on the Santa Fe Trail, and it didn't go so well for him. I reckon he lost some drovers and a slew of cattle. So I ain't afraid of him or you, Red."

"You dang sure should be afraid of me, McLeod. I'm the man who will kill you," Red said.

Trent chuckled. "Maybe, but not today. Now tell your ranch hands to drop their pistols on the floor or else I shoot you where you stand."

Red hesitated.

"Okay, it's your choice," Trent said.

"Do what the sodbuster says, fellows. We'll string him up from the hanging tree at a later date."

The sounds of guns hitting the floor echoed through the room.

"Bartender, you reach for that scattergun, and you'll be in boot hill before the sun sets," Trent said.

The bartender raised his hands and stepped back from the bar.

"Bruce, are you ready to ride?"

"Been ready for a while."

"Then mount your horse. I'll be right behind you." Trent said as he reloaded his Sharps. "Now, in case you galoots don't know it, this is a .50 caliber buffalo rifle. I can kill a man at fifteen hundred yards. So think about that before you straddle your horses and ride after us," Trent said as he backed to the door. "Red, I'll deal with you another time."

With that, Trent backed out of the saloon, spun around, and ran to the edge of the porch. He sprung on the back of Tex.

"Bruce, let's go!" Trent added as he pressed his heels into Tex's sides. The big stallion hit a full gallop in a few strides.

"Dang it," Bruce said. "I hoped I would never hear the name McGregor again. I can't believe we're homesteading near his ranch."

"Believe it," Trent said.

"And here I thought all our troubles were behind us when we left the wagon train," Bruce said, shaking his head.

Chapter Two
Apaches

Trent pulled up as they approached the Canadian River. "We're being watched."

"That same one who shadowed us on our way to Salt Flats?" Bruce asked.

Trent shook his head. "No. More than one this time. I don't know how many, but I'm guessing about twenty."

"Are they going to attack?"

Before Trent had time to answer, a group of Apaches rode out from behind an outcropping of rocks and surrounded Trent and Bruce.

"Don't reach for your pistol," Trent warned.

Bruce nodded.

As a big Apache with a white headband walked up to stand in front of Tex, Trent made the sign of greeting. The big-armed Apache returned the sign, and Trent made several more signs.

"What are you telling him?" Bruce asked.

"I'm telling him we mean him and his people no harm, that we're settling in the valley near the canyons."

"Hmm, he doesn't look too pleased to hear that," Bruce said.

Trent exchanged more signs with the Apache. "Bruce, he says if he brings the white man with cattle our scalps, he'll give them twenty cows."

"Well, I guess we know our worth to McGregor," Bruce said.

"I asked him if twenty cows was worth him losing his life and a handful of men," Trent said.

"What was his answer?"

"His name is Red Hawk, the chief. He says the Kiowa told him of the man who never misses with the long rifle. Red Hawk said he would allow us to live in peace as long as we don't hunt game beyond this point. He said he needs all his hunting ground to feed his people since the buffalo are scarce. I told him we would honor his wish."

Trent exchanged more signs before the Apache turned and led his men back into the rocks.

"He says the cattleman will drive us from the river. That's why he's not in a rush to confront us." Trent sighed. "I told him we would not be driven from our land by either the Apaches or McGregor. And he said I was a brave man or a stupid one."

"Hmm, which are we?" Bruce said.

"I guess a little of both."

"Let's keep McGregor and the Apache meeting from the women. I don't want them getting upset," Bruce said.

"Yeah, you know how Becky gets," Trent replied.

Bruce shook his head. "They melted into those rocks like ghosts."

"Yup, you never see an Apache unless he wants you to see him," Trent said as he urged Tex upriver.

"We just filed our petition for a homestead, and already we have a slew of enemies," Bruce said.

"I'm glad Pat, Wes, and Pony Boy are still with us," Trent said. "That gives us enough guns to make any effort to drive us off the land costly."

"Trent, we must avoid a showdown with both the Apaches and McGregor. I didn't bring my family from Boston to get them killed while I'm settling on my homestead."

"Bruce, I ain't going to let nothing happen to you or your family," Trent vowed.

Bruce smiled. "Yeah, son, I have faith in you and your brother. You got us this far when the odds were stacked against us. I guess you can do it again."

They traveled in silence until they came in sight of the two wagons. "One day, I'll have a log cabin on the spot where the wagons are parked," Bruce said.

"I say we mark trees to cut tomorrow," Trent said as he spotted Becky and her mother working around the cook fire. "Hmm, I'm hungry enough to eat a skunk."

Bruce chuckled as they dismounted.

"So, Pa, did you and Trent file for your homesteads?" Becky asked as she hurried over.

"Yes, honey, we did. This land is now mine... or will be in five years if the Lord is willing and the creek don't rise."

"Tomorrow, Becky, I will take Wes into the woods and start marking trees to cut," Trent said.

Becky shook her head. "When I stop and think of all the work it will take to build a house, I shudder."

Trent shook his head. "Work is good for a man."

"Speak for yourself," Wes said as he walked over. "I hate work. That's why I will not stay and farm with Pa."

"Where is Pat?" Trent asked.

Wes shook his head. "He's over with Pony Boy tending the sheep. I swear if I don't watch it, he will turn into a sheepherder like Pony Boy."

"Becky, I'll see you at supper," Trent said. "Come on, Wes, let's fetch Pat."

Lobo greeted Trent as though he hadn't seen him in a month of Sundays. The big brute jumped and yelped until Trent patted him on the head. Pup ran up to him and sniffed his boots.

"She's only Pony Boy's dog. She doesn't care for nobody else," Pat said. "So, what brings you away from Becky? I know it's not your love of sheep." Pat added.

Trent waved Pony Boy over. He waited until the Arapaho man joined them. "McGregor's spread is downriver from us. I would say a couple of day's ride from what I've gathered from jawing with a sodbuster named Joshua in the saloon.

Pat touched the handles of his pistols but didn't speak.

"With the help of the Apaches, McGregor has been running settlers out of the Canadian River basin.

"I thought he was making the cattle drive to Cheyenne?" Wes said.

Trent nodded. "Luckily, he is, or else things would come to a head quickly. We've got time to get the cabin up so Bruce can make a legitimate claim he's improving the land and entitled to the homestead."

"But someone like McGregor can't just ride up and drive a homesteader off his claim," Wes said.

"It ain't legal, but you can bet the pot that McGregor has the Salt Flat's sheriff and judge in his shirt pocket. If push comes to shove, they will side with McGregor."

"I should have slipped into his camp and killed him when I had a chance," Pat said.

"Well, that would have put your face on a wanted poster, Pat," Trent said.

"Pony Boy kill him," Pony Boy announced.

Trent shook his head. "You ain't killing nobody, Pony Boy." Trent glanced at Pat. "I ran into McGregor's gunslinger. He's as dangerous of a man as I've met. He's got that natural quickness that I've seen in few men. I got the better of him, but it was pure luck. If I had braced him face to face, I'd be in a pine box now."

"Trent, is he that dangerous?" Wes asked.

"Yup. And, Pat, I suspect he might be even faster on the draw than you. So I want you to avoid a showdown when you two meet, as I'm sure you will sooner or later," Trent said.

"I've never backed down to anyone, Trent. I reckon I probably can't do it with this gunslinger. What's his name?"

"Red. He's got red hair and a face full of freckles," Trent said. "He's easy to recognize."

Pat just nodded.

"Wes, we need to keep this under our hats. I don't want to upset your sister. And she'll be fit to be tied if she finds out we're settling near McGregor."

Wes nodded. "Yeah, she will at that."

Trent sighed. "It's about time for supper. Let's all go eat."

"Pa, we need to buy some chickens and pigs," Becky said as Trent and the others arrived at the wagons.

"Yes," Lois said. We need to make a lean-to and unload the wagons. Then you can drive them to Salt Flats and buy some chickens and pigs."

"And a milk cow," Becky said.

Bruce exchanged glances with Trent. "Yeah, well, there's no rush. Let's get the cabin built first."

Trent breathed a sigh of relief. The last thing he wanted was to drive two wagons into Salt Flats for supplies so soon after his confrontation with Red. Trent didn't fear Red, or dying for that matter. However, he wanted to see Bruce's cabin built before taking a one-way trip to boot hill.

"Wes and I'll take one wagon and fetch what you need," Pat spoke up. "That way, Bruce and Trent can start cutting trees."

Trent objected, but Pat stared at him so intently that Trent said nothing.

Bruce shrugged. "Okay."

Trent sought Pat and Wes after supper. "Don't let anyone know you're coming from the Canadian River. If they ask, tell them you're coming from the north. In fact, circle town and come in from the north and leave that way."

"Trent," Pat said. "I've never seen you afraid before."

Trent shook his head. "Pat, you know I'm not afraid for myself. But darn it, I've got to protect Becky. This McGregor is no one to fiddle around with. He's rich and has a slew of ranch hands at his beck and call. Luckily, McGregor is heading to Cheyenne. But that doesn't mean this Red fellow won't take matters in his own hands and try to drive us off our homesteads if he knows where to look. I didn't tell anyone but the sodbuster, Joshua, that we're on the river near the canyons."

"Okay, I'll take care and hide our tracks like a good little Yaqui," Pat said before he turned and walked away.

"What's eating Pat?" Wes asked.

"He's very protective of me," Trent said. "And he's chomping at the bit to brace Red."

As Trent turned to head back toward the wagon, the bark on the ponderosa pine he was standing beside splintered as the loud crack of a rifle echoed through the pines. Trent dropped to the ground and brought his rifle to his shoulder. He scanned the direction of the shot through the sight of his Sharps, but didn't see any movement.

He did see Pony Boy, knife drawn, advance on the area from where the shot came. "That darn fool will get himself killed," Trent mumbled under his breath. He glanced up at the pine. The bullet had missed him by a horse's hair. If he hadn't turned when he did, he would be toes up on the ground now. As Pony Boy disappeared in the underbrush, Trent continued to scan for the shooter.

"Do you see him?" Pat called out from behind a tree nearby.

"Nope. I got nothing to shoot at."

"I guess I have to flush him out. Be ready to shoot when I make a dash for that oak tree," Pat said.

Trent shook his head. "You will get your fool self killed."

Without further comment, Pat made a mad dash for the oak. He ran in a zigzag pattern instead of a straight line.

Suddenly, the dirt kicked up next to Pat's right boot as the sound of a rifle shot echoed through the trees.

Trent was ready. He saw the puff of gunpowder and spotted the man. The shooter had his rifle leaning against the trunk of a pine tree about seventy-five yards from Trent. As Trent watched the man cock his Winchester for another shot, he fired the Sharps. Even before the loud sound of the rifle shot died, Trent started walking toward the shooter.

"Did you get him?" Pat called out.

"Yup," Trent said. "Now, let's look at the bushwhacker."

Before they reached the man, Pony Boy stepped out from a grove of gooseberries. "Two of them. One with the horses. Never saw Pony Boy. Now never see anything," he said.

"You did good," Trent said.

Wes ran up. "Is anyone hurt?"

Trent shook his head. "Just the two bushwhackers. But they aren't hurt. They're dead. Where's Bruce?"

"He's covering Sis and Mama," Wes said. "Who took a shot at you?"

"Come along and let's see," Trent said as he continued to where the man lay unmoving. When he approached the body, Trent stopped. "Well, I'll be. It's Joshua, the sodbuster who warned Bruce and me about McGregor."

"Hmm, that means he played the sodbuster act just to pump you for information, Trent. And he succeeded," Wes said as he walked over while Trent and Pat stared down at the dead man.

Trent nodded. "And it means Red knows our location too.

"What do we do with the bodies?" Wes asked.

"We bury them. I'll get a shovel."

"Come on. Let's see if Lobo and Pup are taking care of the sheep instead of eating them," Pat said. "I don't dig graves."

"Wes, you stay with the bodies," Trent said. "I don't want vultures attacking them, or coyotes."

Bruce met Trent as he approached the wagons. "Why all the shooting?"

"You remember that sodbuster named Joshua who warned us about McGregor?" Trent said.

"Yeah, he was a nice fellow."

"Well, that pleasant fellow tried to kill me," Trent said.

"Why would he do that?"

Trent shrugged. "I guess he works for McGregor to avoid getting kicked off his homestead."

"You know, that explains how Red came rushing in the saloon after you knocked that buckaroo Leroy out with the butt of your rifle. Joshua told him about the incident the moment he walked out of the saloon."

"Yup, I guess he did at that. We thought he was spilling the beans on Mister McGregor when he was just getting close to us so he could find out the location of our homestead," Trent said.

Bruce shook his head. "He was a sneaky coyote."

"Yup. And when he doesn't report back to Red, he'll know something went wrong. He might send others to bushwhack us, Bruce."

"If what Joshua said is correct, and he drives his herd along the Canadian, he'll never tolerate us claiming a homestead here," Bruce said. He sighed. "Maybe we should move on. Head to California."

"No, we filed for a homestead, and we aren't going to let a rich cowpuncher like Cord McGregor drive us off our homestead," Trent said.

Chapter Three
The Homestead

Trent paused as he returned from the river with a bucket of water and looked at the sixteen-by-sixteen-foot log cabin.

Bruce had chosen a clearing among towering ponderosa pines twenty yards from the bank of the Canadian River. The cabin faced the west. From the two windows on each side of the door, you could see the river. Tanned deerskin covered the windows until they could get glass panes. A window on the back side of the cabin provided cross-ventilation. Bruce built the stone chimney on the south side of the cabin.

Trent took a deep breath as he recalled the two months of intense work that had gone into the construction of the log cabin. First had been selecting the trees, next cutting them down, then debarking them. Trent, Wes, and Pat had sweated alongside Bruce, getting the logs ready. It had been backbreaking work. However, the next step, hauling the logs to the site, had been easier. The oxen had done the work.

Once the logs were on site, they had notched them and started stacking them one on top of one another. Lifting the logs had been brutal. The higher they stacked them, the harder it had been to lift the logs. However, with the additional help of Pony Boy taken away from his shepherd duties, they had prevailed in raising the walls.

Bruce, being a former brick mason, had built the chimney with the help of Trent, Pat, and Wes, who had to bring rocks from the river for the fireplace. Bruce cemented the stones together using clay and ash. He had made a similar mixture but added straw for sealing the spaces between the logs.

To Trent's eyes, the log cabin was a beautiful sight. Smoke curled up from the chimney. The smell of fresh biscuits and venison stew drifted through the windows to make his mouth water.

"Trent, are you going to stand there all day wool-gathering, or are you going to bring me the water?" Becky called out from the doorway.

"Just admiring the cabin."

"Yeah, I didn't think I would like it. But I do," Becky said as she held the door open.

Trent sat the bucket on a homemade table against the wall next to the fireplace. Bruce had built the table out of split pine logs, the same as he had used for the long kitchen table and chairs. The west end of the cabin had a pine log bed. Bruce had added a loft with two beds over the entire west end of the cabin. A ladder at the south side gave easy access to the upper level.

"Sit and eat," Bruce called out. He sat at the head of a table. On the north side of the table sat Wes, Pat, and Pony Boy. Lois sat on the south side with an empty chair for Becky next to her. "I guess we should take one of the wagons and ride up to Salt Flats for supplies," Bruce said as he watched Trent take his seat at the other end of the table.

"Yup, but I'll take Pat with me. Things could get dicey if we run into Red." Trent didn't want to mention McGregor's name since they hadn't told Becky the man owned a spread nearby.

"What about this Red fellow, Pa? Has he given you trouble," Becky asked.

Trent answered before Bruce had a chance. "He's a hired hand of a cattle baron that don't like settlers. The local cattlemen association objects to folks homesteading their free grazing land." Trent paused. "I think it's best if Pat and I go for supplies in case there's trouble with any of the ranchers."

"Trent," Becky said. "Don't you go and get yourself shot again. I ain't hankering to sew you up a second time."

"Miss Becky," Pat said with a mouthful of biscuit. "I won't let anyone shoot him."

Becky nodded as she sat down beside her mother. "You better see that you don't."

Becky's concern for him caused Trent to smile and then blush when he noticed everyone looking at him.

Later, as Trent and Pat hitched a pair of Morgan mares to one wagon, Bruce walked over. "Are you sure you don't want me to join you, Trent?"

Trent shook his head. "Nope. I can't risk you getting hurt in a dustup. Lois and Becky would have my head!"

Bruce shook his head. "Okay, but you two stay out of trouble."

As the wagon was fixing to pull away from the cabin, Wes walked over. "Are you sure you don't want me to go with you?"

Trent shook his head. "Nope. You stay and watch over everyone. Keep your eyes peeled for Apaches and McGregor's men while we are away."

"Yeah, I reckon it's getting about time for him to return from the cattle drive," Wes said.

"Yup, but he doesn't know we're here, just that some settlers showed up in Salt Flats and filed for homesteads," Trent said.

Wes shook his head. "Trent, all he has to do is go ask the land agent where you and Pa filed homestead claims," Wes pointed out.

Trent nodded in agreement. "I suppose you're right. But even if he's returned from the cattle drive, I doubt he'll be in Salt Flats."

"Let's hope so," Wes said as he motioned the wagon to continue.

Trent and Pat left the river valley and headed across the drier, flat prairie of short grass. Trent stared ahead.

"What are you looking for?" Pat asked. He held the reins of the team of Morgan mares, freeing Trent up to bring the Sharps to bear should they encounter anything.

"Nothing in particular."

"I feel someone is watching us," Pat said.

Trent nodded. "Yup. Someone is watching us! I would prefer it to be Apaches instead of McGregor's men. The Apaches are honorable. I can't say the same about McGregor."

Pat nodded his head, "Yup, neither can I."

They rode another hour before four men rode out from a dry wash and blocked their passage.

"Howdy," Trent called out as he shifted his rifle in the crook of his arm.

"What are you carrying in the wagon?" one man asked as he rubbed his chin with his left hand while keeping his other hand near his pistol grip. He had a narrow face with a hawk nose and beady eyes.

"Nothing. It's empty. We're headed to town for supplies," Trent replied. "Take a gander if you wish."

"Caleb, ride around and look-see in the back," the man said. He nodded at Trent. "What are y'all doing out here in Apache country?"

Pat twitched in his seat as though he had had enough of the questions.

"Going to Salt Flats for supplies," Trent said and forced a smile.

"You homestead along the river?" the man asked.

"Maybe," Trent answered, a little curt.

"Wagon's empty, Owens," Caleb, a skinny man with an unusually enormous head, called out as he rode back to join the others.

Owens glanced at Trent. "I have a homestead up the river, maybe we're neighbors."

Trent shifted his Sharps in the crook of his arm. "Then a word to the wise, neighbor. You ever stop my wagon again and search it, you'll be in boot hill before nightfall."

Pat turned in the wagon seat so Owens had an unobstructed view of his two Colt Navies.

"You let him wear irons?" Owens asked.

"He's my brother," Trent said. "Now, if you gentlemen will excuse us, we'll be moseying on to Salt Flats."

Pat took that moment to slap the reins against the two Morgans' backs. The wagon lurched forward, forcing Owens's horse to sidestep out of their path.

The four men watched in silence as Pat drove the wagon past them.

"I was fixing to kill the crooked-nosed man," Pat said.

"Yup. But we can't shoot men who aren't outlaws. If we do, there will be a bounty on our heads."

"That's the only thing that swayed my hand, Trent."

"Where do you think this Owens has his homestead? We're upriver," Trent pointed out.

"It won't be healthy for him if his place is close to Bruce's homestead," Pat replied.

"At least he wasn't one of McGregor's men," Trent said.

Trent had Pat circle town and entered Salt Flats from the north instead of the south. They sighted a small white church with a tall steeple as they entered town.

"Maybe you'll have use of the church one of these days," Pat said as he drove past.

Trent smiled but kept silent.

They passed the Cattleman's Saloon and saw a dozen horses tied to the hitching post. "Looks busy," Trent said as Pat drove over to the general store.

Four men lounged on the porch of the store. They perked up at the sight of the wagon. One pushed off from his position leaning against the storefront and walked over to the edge of the porch.

"Y'all coming from the north?" he called out.

"Yup," Trent said. "Had a hard time deciding whether to drive to Salt Flats or Dumas. I had to flip a coin, as I couldn't decide."

The man spat a stream of brown tobacco juice onto the dirt. "Good luck on that, sodbuster. But you might be better putting the barrel of your pistol in your mouth. It'll be a quicker death than working yourself to death on a bone-dry homestead," the man said.

"We didn't have a choice. I heard that ranchers around these parts don't cotton to settlers along the Canadian River."

"Yup, you sure heard that right. Mr. McGregor considers the entire river valley his property."

Trent climbed down off the wagon. "Yup, that's what I heard." He waited for Pat to join him.

"Is he an Apache?" the man asked as he seemed to notice Pat for the first time.

"No, he's half Yaqui, same as me," Trent said in a cold tone that got the man's attention.

"Those are some fancy pistols, Yaqui," the man said.

"Better to shoot white men with," Pat said. Suddenly the pistols appeared in Pat's hands. He twirled them back into his holsters.

"Dang it, Will, he's as fast as Red," one man called out.

"Shut your trap!" Will said.

Trent shifted his rifle. "Gents, we have business inside, if you will excuse us." Trent didn't wait for a response. He walked past the four men in a dismissive manner, with Pat right behind him.

"Trent, I seemed to remember Texas being a more friendly place when we were growing up," Pat said as they entered the store.

Trent shook his head. "Nope, you were too young to realize they were treating us as half-breeds. But I heard the talk behind our backs."

"What can I help you, gentlemen..." the clerk's voice trailed off when he saw Pat.

"We need supplies. I have a list," Trent said and handed the clerk the list that Becky had written out for her parents.

"You got money? I don't give sodbusters credit," the middle-aged man said.

Pat reached into his pocket and pulled out a wad of Lincolns. "Yup."

The clerk's eyes widened at the size of the wad. He cleared his throat. "If you'll hand me the list, I'll see if I have all the items listed."

Trent handed the man the list without a word. Then he and Pat wandered around the store, picking items that grabbed their fancy. When they finished, they had four large boxes stacked on the floor in front of the counter.

The four loafers watched while Trent, Pat, and the store clerk loaded the boxes into the wagon. They watched in sullen silence as Trent and Pat climbed into the wagon seat. Will stepped off the porch and walked behind the wagon for a way as though to confirm they were heading back north.

"Trent, McGregor has this town under his boot. I hope Bruce never needs the sheriff of Salt Flats to help in a beef against McGregor. If he does, Bruce is going to come up with the short end of the stick. And you know, eventually, I will have to kill McGregor."

Trent shook his head. "No, it can't come to that. He's a powerful man in Texas. You would hang."

Pat slapped the reins against the back of the horses. As the wagon pulled out of Salt Flats, Trent spotted a flock of chickens milling around in the front yard of a shack. "Pat, pull over, I want to see if I can buy Becky some chickens."

Half an hour later, they continued on home, this time with five hens and a rooster with their legs tied together in the back of the wagon.

"Looks like we'll have eggs to go with our biscuits in the mornings from now on," Pat said as he finally turned the wagon south.

Chapter Four
Neighbors

Trent wiped the sweat off his brow with his bandana after he marked the last tree for cutting. His trees, for his log cabin. He had it in the back of his mind to ask Becky to marry him once they raised the cabin.

His homestead site lay downriver from Bruce's, on a high riverbank, only ten yards from the river. With the height of the riverbank, Trent felt safe building the cabin so close to the Canadian. Even in an extreme flood, the thirty-foot cliff should protect the cabin.

He felt a thrill surge through him at the thought of he and Becky sharing the log cabin. He let out a sigh. Between now and raising the cabin lay a lot of back-breaking work for everyone. However, for Trent, it would be a labor of love.

Trent had just picked up his rifle he had leaned against one pine tree when he heard a horse approaching. He turned around to find Owens staring at him from atop a piebald gelding.

"Pardner, what are you doing on my land?" Owens asked in a bitter tone.

Trent shook his head. "Ain't yours. I filed a claim on this quarter of a section months ago."

"I have taken it. I filed on it six years back. Just been away, taking care of business," Owens said.

Trent shrugged. "I've got the paperwork on my filing. Do you?"

Owens glared at Trent in silence.

"Well?" Trent asked again.

"Lost it. But that doesn't mean anything. I filed first. This is my property."

Trent shook his head. "I don't see it that way, and neither with the land claim office. You have made no improvements to the land. No house at the end of five years, no claim," Trent said as he shifted the rifle in the crook of his arm, ready to use it. The homestead was his, and he would kill anyone who tried to claim otherwise.

Owens noticed when Trent shifted the rifle. His eyes narrowed but then returned to normal. "I ain't going to give up my claim!"

"There's plenty of land near the river. Find another spot," Trent said.

"Nope, this had the best view of the river and the valley. I don't want another spot," Owens said.

Trent shook his head. "Now, that's tough because the only way you will take this claim from me is if'n my toes are turned up."

"That could happen, pardner," Owens said.

Trent smiled. "Maybe, but not here and now. You best mosey on from wherever you came from. My patience is thin today."

"You dang sure haven't seen the last of me," Owens said before he reined his gelding around and rode back the way he had come.

Trent shouldered his rifle and headed back to Bruce's cabin. He brooded over the other mans claim that he had filed on the homestead site before him. But it eased his mind a bit that Owens didn't have his signed claim papers from the land office. If push came to shove, Trent thought he would win since Owens didn't have a title.

"You look worried," Bruce said when Trent entered the cabin.

"What are you building?" Trent asked instead of answering the question.

"Some shelves for Lois. She says she doesn't have any place to store dishes," Bruce replied. "So you want to tell me what caused that worried look on your face?"

Trent glanced around. "Where are the women?"

"At the river doing laundry. Why?"

"You remember those four men Pat and I ran into when we drove the wagon to Salt Flats?"

Bruce nodded. "Yeah, they searched the wagon."

"I ran into the leader, a man named Owens, as I finished marking the last tree I want to cut for the cabin," Trent explained.

"Yeah, and what happened? Owens must have said something to give you that worried look."

Trent took a deep breath. "He said he filed on my homestead site six years ago."

Bruce looked surprised. "He did?"

"Yup. But he said he lost the papers."

Bruce shook his head. "It doesn't matter if he has the claim or not. You have to make improvements to the land before the end of the fifth year, or your claim is void." Bruce shook his head again. "I don't see any signs that a man has set foot on your quarter section of land."

"Nope, neither do I," Trent agreed.

"Is this Owens going to be trouble?"

Trent nodded. "Yup."

"Trent, be careful. It's one thing to kill outlaws, but another to kill a man over a dispute. Doing that will get you hanged."

"That's about what I told Pat. Bruce, I know Pat is chomping at the bit to confront Red. I've got to keep it from happening," Trent said.

"Because you think this Red fellow might be quicker on the draw?" Bruce asked.

"I guess it's a little of that, but I'm concerned that, even if it's a duel and he kills Red, he might be arrested and tried for murder since he's Yaqui and looks it."

"Yeah, folks in these parts don't like Indians killing whites."

"Hello in there!"

Trent instantly recognized the voice as belonging to Owens. He grabbed his rifle. "It's the fellow I was telling you about, Bruce. He's here," Trent said as he walked over and opened the door. He stepped outside. "It's my unlucky day to see you twice," Trent called out as he stared at the four mounted men.

"Yeah, I guess it is at that, blondie."

"What can I do for you, gentlemen?" Bruce said as he joined Trent.

"You can tell your blond friend to stay off my property," Owens said.

Bruce shook his head. "That's the rub, sir. It ain't your land. It belongs to Trent. He filed a homestead claim on it."

"I filed one on the property six years ago. It's mine, I tell you," Owens said as his horse got a little spooky and turned in a circle. "Hold still, you dang bangtail," Owens shouted as he jerked savagely on the reins. The horse nickered and backed up.

"That's no way to treat a horse," Pat said as he walked up behind the four men.

Owens and the others turned in their saddles.

"It's the two-gun Yaqui," Caleb said.

"The man's got a memory," Pat said. "We usually look alike to you white people."

"Are you making fun of me, boy?" Caleb demanded. He glanced at Owens. "Is he making fun of me?" he asked.

"Yup," Owens said.

Caleb reached for his iron. Before his hand touched his pistol grip, a bullet shattered the handle of the Colt.

Pat twirled his right pistol back into his holster. "Yup, I made fun of you," Pat said in a calm voice. "And I think the four of you have overstayed your welcome."

Trent nodded. "Yup, I agree with my younger brother. It's time for you gents to head for the hills. And I would appreciate it if you didn't return."

Owens pointed his finger at Trent. "I ain't gonna let someone steal my homestead! You can put that in your skillet and cook it!" Owens nodded to his men. "Come on," he said as he turned his horse around. Owens glanced back at Trent. "I'll be back," he added before he urged his horse into a trot.

Bruce shook his head. "That man's got outlaw written all over him."

Trent nodded. "Yup, and we ain't seen the last of him."

Bruce shook his head. "We just can't seem to outrun trouble."

"What trouble, Pa?" Becky asked as she walked up, carrying a wicker basket full of freshly washed clothes.

Bruce shook his head. "Nothing to concern you, just an old ornery neighbor."

Becky glanced at Trent. "I didn't know we had neighbors."

Trent shook his head. "Neither did I."

"We should invite him and his wife over for dinner," Becky said.

Bruce shook his head. "It ain't a couple. It's four tough-looking men. They don't have a homestead filed yet, and there's a good chance they won't stay."

"Four men, that's strange," Becky said as she carried the laundry into the cabin.

Trent waited until Becky disappeared into the house. "Pat, let's track Owens and his men. I want to see where they're camping," Trent said as he headed for the corral to get Tex.

The big palomino stallion nickered and bobbed his head to show his eagerness to get out of the enclosure. Trent made quick work of saddling Tex. He wasn't too concerned about losing Owens's trail. Pat was one of the best trackers,

Trent knew. And anyway, tracking four horses wouldn't be difficult.

"They might expect us to follow them," Pat said as they rode away from the cabin.

Trent shrugged. "We'll keep our eyes peeled."

"Okay," Pat said as he took the lead. He bent over and studied the ground as they rode away from the cabin. "It's easy to track them here. They're heading up into the canyons. It might get more difficult."

"Why would they head for the canyons?" Trent asked.

"Maybe they have a place up there," Pat replied. "They aren't hiding their tracks."

"They feel confident they can lose anyone who trails them up in the rocks. If they were on Indian ponies they might but not on shoed horses," Trent said.

"Yup, their horses' iron shoes will leave marks on the rocks. It'll be slow going, but I should be able to track them," Pat said.

"We'll know soon," Trent said as they emerged from a stand of ponderosa pines and entered a rocky incline.

Moments later, Pat slid off Leo and walked in front of his horse. He stopped every so many steps to kneel and study the rocky ground before he motioned for Trent to continue.

"I see passageways branching off in all directions," Trent called out. "No wonder they didn't hide their tracks. It would take a Yaqui to track them in this terrain," Trent said with a chuckle.

Pat glanced back. "It ain't easy."

"Yeah, but you are the best," Trent called back.

"Trent, what are you going to do if this Owens fellow pushes his claim on your land?"

Trent shook his head. "Let hope it doesn't come to that. Salt Flats is McGregor's town. He probably has the sheriff in his pocket. When McGregor learns we've settled along the Canadian River, he will be fit to be tied. He will try to drive us off the homestead in a legal effort." Trent shook his head. "However, if that fails, he'll use force."

Pat held up his hand. Trent pulled on Tex's reins stopping, the stallion.

Pat pointed to a narrow path between two towering walls of rock. "They rode into that canyon. What do you want to do?"

"Let's hide the horses in case someone else comes this way and go on foot," Trent said as he dismounted. "The group of rocks on the left will do. We'll tie the horses behind it."

Pat followed Trent behind the rocks where they tied the horses to a stunted pine.

"They must be outlaws to have a secret hideout," Pat said as they followed the path toward the canyon.

The length of the entrance to the box canyon surprised Trent. When they finally emerged from a passageway wide enough for only one horse at a time, Trent found a small canyon with stunted cedar trees and pines.

"Over there," Pat whispered as he pointed to the left.

"A lean-to," Trent said when he spotted the logs leaned against the wall of the canyon. It looked as though they had sealed the logs of the building to keep out the rain. "A good idea to build something simple like that. I'm guessing they cut down most of the larger cedar trees in the canyon to build it."

Pat nodded beyond the lean-to. "They have a corral for their horses. It means they've used this place often."

"This explains why they don't want me homesteading nearby. Owens wants to come and go without being seen," Trent said.

Pat nodded. "That also means they are outlaws."

"This eases my mind some. If the men are outlaws, we have to locate wanted posters on them, and then we can arrest Owens and his men and take them to the sheriff in Salt Flats," Trent said.

"That means another trip to town. And you know the welcome wagon isn't out for us," Pat said.

Trent shrugged. "We can't homestead and never visit Salt Flats. We got to face McGregor sooner or later."

"What do you want to do now?" Pat asked.

"We got what we came for, let's head back to the cabin. I don't want Owens to catch us spying on him. Let him think his hideout is safe," Trent said as he doubled over and hurried back the way they had come.

Chapter Five
The Sheriff

Trent swung the ax hard. The blade bit deep into the pine, sending wood chips flying. Trent lifted the ax over his shoulder to take another swing at the tree, but paused.

Horses!

He laid the ax against the tree and walked over to pick up his rifle. He had just lifted it to the crook of his arm when seven riders broke from the cedar thicket.

Owens!

The hawk-nosed man spotted Trent and turned his horse in his direction. The other riders followed him and surrounded Trent.

"I didn't give you permission to cut my trees, pardner," Owens said as he glanced at his men as though to say, *Who's got the upper hand now?*

"We've had this discussion twice before, Owens. It ain't going to come out any different this time. I filed a homestead claim on this section, and it's mine," Trent said as he shifted the Sharps in the crook of his arm.

"Your buffalo rifle don't scare me none. It's a single shot."

Trent shrugged. "That's all I need to put you in the dirt."

Owens suddenly got a nervous look on his face. He cleared his throat. "You'd be dead before you could reload."

"Have you had your eyes checked? I think you might need spectacles," Trent said.

Owens looked puzzled.

"You seem not to have seen the Colt I'm packing," Trent said.

"Yeah, boss, he's got a fine Colt Army," Caleb said.

"Shut your trap. I didn't ask you anything," Owens snapped. He nodded at Trent. "If you're so good with a pistol, why are you hugging the rifle all the time?"

Trent shrugged his shoulders. "I favor the long gun. But that doesn't mean I'm not handy with a pistol."

"You're bluffing. You're probably slow as molasses," Owens said.

"Fly to it and find out. But I'll send you to boot hill along with at least three of your men." Trent nodded at the skinny man with the pumpkin head. "Caleb, are you willing to die to keep me from cutting a tree on my homestead?"

Caleb looked at Owens. "Boss?"

Owens didn't answer for a long moment. "You're lucky I'm in a hurry. I've got business up in Dumas. But another time, things might have a different outcome."

"Yeah, you might be heading for boot hill when we meet again," Trent said. "Now I've got work to do. This pine tree won't chop itself down. So have a go at it or ride off to Dumas!"

"Let's go, boss," Caleb called out.

Several more riders nodded their heads to support Caleb. Trent saw Owens grind his teeth in frustration.

"Soon," Owens said. "You and I will lock horns, and one of us ain't walking away."

Trent didn't reply while he watched the men ride off toward the canyon country. He smiled to himself because he knew where they were headed.

Trent resumed chopping down the tree. After he felled it, he moved on to the next one he had marked. Trent worked until sweat dripped down the front of his blue and white plaid shirt before stopping for the day. He whistled for Tex. The stallion who had enjoyed grazing in a meadow nearby, trotted up eagerly.

"We ain't going for a run. Just back to the cabin," Trent said as he mounted.

Becky spotted him from the window of the cabin and hurried out to greet him. "I was fixing to send Lobo to find you," she said.

Trent shook his head. "I reckon you won't be able to drag him away from the flock of sheep long enough to fetch me. He thinks the sheep belong to him and Pup."

"Yeah, I reckon you're right. I ain't seen anything like it. A wolf-dog adopting a flock of sheep."

"Yup, and Pony Boy has adopted them too. We don't see hide nor hair of him until mealtime."

When Trent followed Becky into the cabin, he found everyone, including Pony Boy, seated at the table.

"We were waiting for you to serve supper," Bruce said as Lois dipped venison stew into everyone's bowls.

Trent took his seat at the other end of the table. "I ran into Owens today. He had more men with him," Trent said and didn't elaborate. He glanced at Pat as he spoke.

Pat nodded. "I reckon it's about time to head back to Salt Flats for supplies."

"Do you want me to go along?" Wes asked with stew running down the corner of his mouth.

"No," Trent replied quickly. "You stay and protect the cabin."

"Trent," Becky asked, "what does Wes need to protect the cabin from?"

"Bears, Apaches, and bandits," Trent rattled off the list.

"Oh," Becky said.

Later, as the men sat outside on a homemade bench made from split logs, Bruce said, "Trent, do you want to tell me what's going on? Why do you need to go to Salt Flats?"

"Owens braced me for cutting down trees. He had six men with him. He said I didn't ask permission to cut his trees."

"You didn't kill anyone, did you?" Bruce asked.

"Nope, but it was touch and go for a moment."

"Is Owens the reason we're going to Salt Flats tomorrow?" Pat asked.

"Yup, we need to go to the sheriff and see if he has any wanted posters on Owens," Trent said.

"And if he does?" Wes asked.

Trent shrugged. "Pat and I will take him to the sheriff."

"He ain't gonna go without kicking," Bruce said.

Pat touched both hands to the grips of his Colts. "Let him. I have a remedy for that."

Bruce shook his head. "Please, let's not kill anyone. I want to live here in peace."

"We might not have a choice," Trent said. "If it's him or me, I will put Owens in the dirt."

Wes stood up. "Y'all get to have all the fun while I stay here babysitting."

"If you're going to cry about it, I'll buy you a pacifier in Salt Flats, Wes," Trent said.

Everyone laughed but Wes, who jumped up from the bench and stalked off.

Bruce shook his head. "There's still a lot of boy in him."

***

Trent and Pat left before daylight. They didn't disturb the Cowan family since they slept in a wagon parked beside the cabin. The second wagon where Pony Boy bunked, had been parked in the big meadow near the sheep. Trent only saw the Arapaho when he came to the cabin for meals. He hardly ever saw Lobo unless he visited the sheep. The big wolf-dog and Pup wouldn't leave the flock.

"Pat, even if there's trouble when we reach Salt Flats, don't kill anyone."

Pat nodded as they walked their horses along the bank of the Canadian.

Once out of the valley, they turned north and increased the pace across the drier, rolling hills, which later flattened out to a prairie of short, stubby, brown grass. Once they neared Salt Flats, they circled and rode in from the north.

The town bustled with activity in the midmorning. Wagons headed out of town, carrying feed to homesteads in the north while other wagons carried supplies to the ranchers south of town. Trent noted that the further north you rode, the drier the land. He felt sorry for the settlers, mostly Polish immigrants.

Men and women strolled along the street, looking into storefronts and shopping. Trent didn't see any ranch hands hanging on the porch of the general store when they rode past. The hitching post in front of the sheriff's office had one horse, a buckskin gelding, tied to it.

Trent and Pat looped the reins of their horses over the hitching post. They exchanged glances before stepping onto the porch. Trent, with his Sharps in the crook of his arm, entered first.

The man in a tan shirt and battered slouch hat jerked his feet off his desk and looked as though he was trying to decide whether to draw his pistol.

"Howdy, Sheriff," Trent called out in a friendly tone. "I didn't mean to interrupt your nap."

"Just resting my eyes, nothing more," the man said. His eyes widened when Pat stepped into the office. "What can I do you for?" the sheriff asked, his hand still down near his pistol grip.

"We came across some men who looked like outlaws on our way to Salt Flats," Trent said. "We wondered if we could take a gander at your wanted posters and see if we recognize them."

"What, you sodbusters are turning into bounty hunters?"

"Times are hard. Every Lincoln counts, Sheriff," Trent said.

"Is he mute?" the sheriff asked, jutting his chin in Pat's direction.

Pat shook his head. "No, I just don't like flapping my lip unless I got something important to say."

The lack of an accent took the sheriff by surprise. He cleared his throat. He pointed to two chairs in front of his desk. "Take a load off."

"Don't mind if I do," Trent said as he and Pat took seats.

The sheriff reached into the side drawer of his desk and pulled out a thick stack of wanted posters. "Here, have a go at it."

Trent took the stack and divided it, handing some to Pat. "Seems to be a lot of wanted men in Texas," Trent said.

"Where are you gents homesteading?"

"North of town," Trent said as he glanced up. Before he resumed shuffling through the posters, he added, "My brother and I haven't been given a very warm welcome in Salt Flats."

"Haven't you two noticed this is cattle country? We don't need sodbusters fencing off the grazing land. It takes a lot of land to graze a big herd of cattle."

"You mean like the spread McGregor owns," Pat said.

"He runs a lot of cattle. He needs a lot of grazing land. His cattle range from the Canadian north toward Dumas. And he especially doesn't like homesteaders settling in the river valley."

"But the Canadian River Valley is open for homesteading. It's legal to settle in the valley," Trent pointed out.

"Trent, this is him," Pat said, holding up a wanted poster.

The sheriff leaned forward to look at the poster. "Why, that's Owens McGill! He's wanted for killing a Texas Ranger and robbing stagecoaches in Dumas and Santa Fe. You're lucky you're still upright after meeting him and his boys."

Pat shook his head. "Nope, he's lucky to be above ground."

The sheriff seemed to notice Pat's two Navies for the first time. "So you say," he finally replied.

"Is the wanted poster correct? Is Owens wanted dead or alive?" Trent said. "And the reward $800?"

The sheriff glanced from Trent to Pat and then back at Trent. "Are you boys sure you're sodbusters?"

Trent nodded. "I am. My brother is just helping me raise the cabin. He's a bounty hunter."

"I ain't never heard of an Indian bounty hunter," the sheriff said.

"It's the only way I can legally kill a white man," Pat said. His face didn't betray a trace of emotion. "And I enjoy it."

The sheriff cleared his throat. "Now, look here. A wanted poster doesn't give you license to gun down a man."

"It does," Pat said. "Or maybe you didn't read the 'dead or alive' printed on the wanted poster." He noticed the sheriff's change in expression. "Yup, I can read and write, sheriff."

"I'll be taking the poster, Sheriff," Trent said. He didn't wait for an answer before he folded it and tucked it in the pocket of his shirt. "Get the reward money ready. We will bring Owens McGill in, though I can't say whether it'll be in the saddle or across it."

The sheriff didn't respond except to stare at them as Trent stood and turned to leave.

He paused just at the door and turned back. "Good day, Sheriff."

"He wasn't much of a sheriff if you ask me," Pat said as they walked over to their horses.

"He's just the kind that a man like McGregor can control. If we get into trouble with McGregor, the sheriff ain't going to side with us, even if we're in the right," Trent said as he mounted Tex. "Let's go to the general store and pick up the list of supplies Bruce wanted."

"All right, but when we finish, I want some whiskey," Pat said, nodding toward the Cattleman's Saloon.

"Are you sure, Pat? It might rile folks up for us to stop in there."

"Since when did you care about getting into trouble?" Pat asked.

"Since I settled down. I will ask Becky to marry me as soon as I raise the cabin."

Pat shook his head. "Wes was right. She's got you roped and hogtied."

Chapter Six
The Cattleman's Saloon

"You sure about this, Pat?" Trent said as they approached the butterfly doors.

"Yup, I need me some firewater!"

Four men played poker at a table near the door: a professional gambler, and three cowpunchers. More men sat at tables scattered around the room, usually two to a table. Several men drank at the bar. One wore a dark suit. Trent headed toward him.

"What'll it be…" the bartender's voice trailed off when he spotted Pat. "We don't—"

Pat cut him off. "Whiskey!" he said, squaring himself to the bartender, so he got a view of his Colts.

The bartender, a fat, bald man with a handlebar mustache, swallowed before he reached for a bottle of whiskey. He didn't take his eyes off Pat as he filled two shot glasses.

"Leave the bottle," Pat said with a straight face.

"Your friend doesn't sound like an Indian," the man in the suit standing next to Trent said. "He's got a perfect Texan accent."

"He's my brother. We were raised in Texas," Trent replied as he held his glass for Pat to refill.

"I see. You can probably tell by my accent that I'm not a Texan. I'm for Philadelphia. My name is Jack Jetson. I'm the preacher over at Heaven's Gate Church—when I'm sober, that is. And I am on Sundays."

"I didn't think Christians drank?" Trent said.

"Depends on the flavor. Most don't, at least not on Sunday. I don't drink on Sunday, but during the week, I give in to temptation. Show me a man who says he is without sin, and I'll show you a liar," Preacher Jetson said.

"I'll drink to that," Pat called out as he tossed a shot of whiskey into his mouth.

"Where's your church?" Trent asked.

"The adobe building east of town. It ain't a white church with a steeple like the one in town. But then that's where the ranchers go. My flock consists of sodbusters and Mexicans. A rancher wouldn't set foot in Heaven's Gate."

"Do you perform weddings?" Trent asked.

Pat choked on his shot of whiskey and started coughing.

"Oh," the preacher said. He cleared his throat. "Why do you ask about weddings? Are you planning on getting hitched?"

Pat turned to face them as he waited for Trent's response.

"Yup. I've got a girl in mind to ask to marry me soon," Trent said as he ignored Pat glaring at him. "I reckon your church might suit me better than the fancy church the ranchers attend."

"Well, son, you just let me know the day, and if it's during the week, I'll make sure I'm sober," Preacher Jetson said as he stared at the bottle of whiskey in front of Pat.

"Ah, do you want a drink?" Trent asked as he reached for the bottle. He nodded at the bartender. "Another glass."

"He ain't no preacher. He's just a drunk," a man in a red shirt and brown chaps said as he walked up to the bar. "That church of his is just a rat's nest of varmints. It should be burned to the ground."

Trent tensed as he squared himself around to face the man. "I don't recall inviting you to join our jawing session, pardner."

"A sodbuster and an Indian! Rufus," the man said as he looked across the bar. "When did you start letting Indians into the Cattleman?"

"Jeremiah, they didn't ask. They just barged in. What could I do?"

"You know Pa doesn't like their kind in the Cattleman, Rufus," the man said.

"Who's your pappy?" Trent asked.

"Cord McGregor, I'm sure you've heard of him. We run more cattle than any other ranch in Texas."

"Yup, I've heard of him, although I can't recall hearing anything good about him," Trent said.

Jeremiah reached for his pistol.

Trent brought the stock of his Sharps up. The butt of the rifle struck the young man under the chin. Jeremiah went suddenly limp. He dropped to the floor.

"You've done it now!" the bartender shouted. He glanced over at the two men sitting at the closest table to the bar. "You two galoots get over here and help Jeremiah up," he shouted.

"What's all the ruckus about?" the sheriff asked as he pushed through the butterfly doors.

The bartender glanced at the door. "Sheriff Givens. The blond knocked out Jeremiah," the bartender called out.

The chubby sheriff hurried up as the two men helped Jeremiah into a chair. "He's still out cold." The sheriff glanced nervously at Trent while he waited for the answer.

"The blond hit him with the butt of his rifle," Rufus said.

"He went for his pistol, Sheriff," Trent said.

The sheriff looked at the bartender. "Is that true, Rufus?"

The bartender hesitated a moment until he saw the look in Trent's eyes. "Yeah, It's true. But the blond insulted Mister McGregor," Rufus said.

"Did you?"

Trent shrugged. "I just told him the truth. I have heard nothing good about his pappy."

"Yeah, well, Jeremiah don't like people badmouthing his father. None of the four McGregor boys do. And they ain't going to be happy that a sodbuster laid hands on their brother."

Trent smiled. "I didn't lay hands on him. I laid into him with the butt of my buffalo rifle."

"Don't get cute with me, son."

Trent shook his head. "I ain't broke the law. A man's got a right to defend himself in Texas. I could have killed him and been within my rights, Sheriff."

Sheriff Givens cleared his throat. "I think it's best if the two of you clear out of town before word reaches Cord you injured his youngest son."

Pat pulled out a wad of bills and peeled one off the roll and slapped it onto the bar. "That should take care of the bottle," he said as he grabbed the whiskey.

Trent turned to Preacher Jetson. "I'll let you know the date of the wedding as soon as I know it."

"You do that. It will be my pleasure to marry you and your lady friend. If you're still alive. You just stirred a hornet's nest," Preacher Jetson said.

Trent smiled. "Preacher, it ain't the first, nor will it be the last hornet's nest I stir." He touched the brim of his hat before turning to follow Pat out of the saloon.

"Well, at least we didn't kill anyone," Pat said as he mounted Leo.

"Not today, at least," Trent agreed as he reined Tex around. "I think we should let them run some," Trent added as he pressed his heels into Tex's side. The big palomino quickly broke into a gallop. They rode hard north for two miles.

"Time we turned south," Pat said as he reined Leo to a stop. He walked over and cut a branch off a cottonwood. He walked back to Trent, who had remained mounted. "Tie the branch onto your saddle horn and pull it behind Tex to wipe out our tracks so we can turn toward home."

"Why me?" Trent protested.

"You know why. Because Tex is a lot calmer than Leo."

Trent smiled. "Yeah, I just want to hear it from your mouth.

"You know they'll try to follow us," Pat said.

"Yup, we hurt the pride of one cattle baron's son. He will be redeye mad," Trent said.

"Yup, just think how mad he would be if he knew it was us that laid his son out cold," Pat said as he climbed back into the saddle.

"Mad enough to swallow a horned toad backwards," Trent said with a chuckle.

An hour later, Trent stopped and untied the cottonwood branch. "I have seen no dust on our trail. I think we're safe from pursuit."

"Yup, unless they bring in one of the Apaches," Pat said.

"Darn, I hadn't thought of that. I guess McGregor could if he's back at the ranch which he should be by now," Trent said.

"So... you've finally decided to marry Becky?" Pat asked.

"There ain't no finally to it, Pat. I made up my mind to marry Becky the moment I laid eyes on her." He shrugged. I've tried to resist. But I'm done ready to surrender."

"I'm happy for you, Trent. But I've got too much sand in my boots to settle down. Wes and I will head on west as soon as we raise your log cabin."

"What about Pony Boy?"

"You've seen him with those sheep. He ain't leaving them. I've lost him the same as you've lost Lobo. That wolf-dog ain't ever leaving Pup and the sheep."

"Yeah, I reckon you're right," Trent admitted.

"You know the ruckus with McGregor's son will make collecting the bounties on Owens difficult. Returning to Salt Flats is asking for trouble," Pat said.

"You are right as rain. However, Pat, sooner or later, we have to confront McGregor. We can't avoid the showdown forever. I just don't want to brace McGregor to get me hanged," Trent said.

"Yup," Pat said. "I want to die in the saddle, blazing away with my Colts and not hanging by the neck from a tree."

"Hmm, I have in mind dying of old age sitting beside Becky outside the cabin watching the sunset," Trent said.

Pat shook his head. "Old age ain't for me. I've seen too many drooling, old men with no teeth. I don't want to join them."

Trent nodded south. "I see trees. We're approaching the river." He scanned the horizon. "We ain't seen no Apaches in a while."

"Yeah, but they've seen us. Someone is watching us," Pat said with a nod to the right.

"They ain't bothering us," Trent said as they continued to the river. As they approached the riverbank, Trent pulled Tex to a stop at the sound of a fast-approaching horse. He prepared himself to use his Sharps, but relaxed a bit when he recognized Wes's Quarter Horse. "I wonder what this is about," he said.

Wes's horse skidded to a stop in front of Trent.

"What's got you riding like the devil is chasing you?" Trent asked.

"It's Pa. A rattlesnake spooked his horse. It reared and fell on his leg. His leg is broke. We've got to get him to a doctor, Trent."

"Dang it!" Trent swore.

"What's the matter?" Wes asked.

Pat answered, "Trent knocked out one of Cord McGregor's sons with the butt of his rifle. We ain't welcome in Salt Flats at the moment."

Wes shook his head. "Dumas is too far. Pa busted his leg something fierce. He needs to see a doctor!"

"Okay, then we'll take him," Trent said. "Let's get going," he added as he kicked his heels into Tex's sides.

Chapter Seven
The Medicine Man

Trent shook his head. "I've made up my mind," he said as he tied Tex to the back of the wagon. "Salt Flats is too far. The trip will be too jarring. It'll damage his leg more. Pat said the Apache camp is only an hour by wagon. The Apache medicine man can doctor Bruce's leg."

Lois wrung her hands as she paced back and forth in front of Bruce in the wagon's bed. "A medicine man?"

"Take me to him, Trent," Bruce said through clenched teeth.

"I'll go with y'all," Wes said.

Pat shook his head. "No, it's better if just Trent and I go. We've met the chief."

"Son, you stay here and watch over your mother and sister," Bruce called out from the wagon.

Wes nodded and stepped back from the wagon as it lurched forward.

"I hope you're right, Trent," Bruce said between grunts as the wagon bounced over the rough ground.

"Trent," Pat called out as he rode beside the wagon. "I'll ride ahead to have a chat with Red Hawk. If we ride up with the wagon, it might spook them. Then anything could happen."

Trent nodded. "Okay, you know best, Pat."

"I hope the Apaches have something for pain," Bruce called out.

"They do. Smoke from a mixture of dried primrose, sage, and tobacco," Trent made up to make his friend feel better. "It'll put you to sleep."

"That will be a blessing," Bruce replied weakly. He fell silent except for grunts of pain each time the wagon lurched over a rock or a rut. Pat had spied on the Apaches and knew the location of their camp. Trent followed the direction his brother had given him.

Trent turned north from the river at the large boulder. Once through a pine forest, Trent spotted the hill and knew the Apache camp lay on the other side. As he drove the wagon up the hill, a group of mounted men, yelling at the top of their lungs, suddenly surrounded the wagon.

Trent ignored them as he drove up the hill. When he topped the summit, he spotted the mass of tipis dotting the valley below. The whooping men escorted the wagon down the hill and among the tipis to one where Pat's spotted mustang stood.

Pat emerged from the tipi along with Chief Red Hawk and an Apache medicine man wearing a mask made from the head of a buffalo.

The medicine man shouted something to some men standing nearby. They hurried to the wagon and climbed into the bed. Bruce screamed when they lifted him out of the wagon.

Bruce's cries of pain caused Trent to grimace. "Pat, tell them to be careful," Trent said.

Pat spoke to the medicine man. The Apache brushed off Pat's comments with a hand gesture that even Trent could understand.

Instead of taking Bruce into the tipi, they carried him past it.

"Pat, where are they taking Bruce?"

"To the sweat lodge."

Trent followed the men, but Pat put his hand on Trent's shoulder. "You can't enter the sweat lodge. Wait at the wagon."

"And you?" Trent asked when he took a few steps toward the wagon and noticed Pat didn't follow him.

"I will smoke the peace pipe with Chief Red Hawk. He doesn't like your blond hair."

"All right," Trent mumbled as he climbed into the wagon seat. While he sat in the wagon, Trent wondered if he should have taken Bruce to Salt Flats. It had never been in his nature to avoid trouble, but here he had done just that.

He didn't fear Red or Cord McGregor and his offspring. He didn't even fear death, but dang it, he wanted to marry Becky and spend some time with her before he made a one-way trip to boot hill. "I guess I've just turned cautious," he mumbled as he grabbed a piece from a burlap sack and used it to polish his rifle.

The men standing near the wagon eyed the buffalo rifle admiringly as he cleaned it. Trent figured they had heard tales from the Kiowa about the accuracy and effective distance of the rifle.

He had long since finished cleaning the Sharps when Pat returned from the sweat lodge. "How's Bruce?" Trent asked.

"Asleep," Pat said as he stepped around a big Apache man to approach the wagon. "We have to leave him in the sweat lodge for two days."

Trent shook his head. "Dang it. Neither Becky nor her ma will like that."

Pat shrugged. "We have to."

"Did the medicine man set his leg?"

Pat shook his head. "No, I did. Once the smoke put Bruce to sleep."

"Pat! You know nothing about setting a bone!"

"I've watched doctors set bones. It ain't that difficult. I would have done it back at the cabin, but I needed him asleep so I could take my time and align the bones properly.

Trent shook his head. "Dang it. I wonder if one of our ancestors was a medicine man?"

Pat shook his head as he mounted Leo. "I don't know."

"Do you think he'll be okay?" Trent asked

"The medicine man treated the break with a poultice, using several types of tree bark and honey to keep down the swelling. Let's hope it works."

Trent shook his head. "Miss Lois will scalp us both when we return without Bruce." Trent sighed, "It's a good thing I tied Tex to the rear of the wagon. We can leave it here and ride back. It'll be quicker."

They didn't talk much as they headed back to the cabin. As they approached the river, Trent held up his hand to signal Pat to stop. He pointed through the pines. Eight men rode single file along the bank of the river.

"Owens McGill," Trent said softly. "They have a packhorse. It looks like two strong boxes strapped on it."

"They must have robbed a train," Pat said. "At least we don't have to follow them. We know where they're headed."

"Owens has picked up more men. His gang is growing. We will have to confront him before he gets so many men we can't take them down," Trent said. "Too bad Bruce is hurt, or I would go after them in the next few days."

"Yup, but we have to take care of Bruce's injury first," Pat said.

Once the riders had cleared out of the area, Trent and Pat continued to the cabin. Becky rushed out of the house to meet them. "Where's Pa?"

"We left him at the Apache camp. They have him in the sweat lodge treating his leg. He's comfortable, Becky. The medicine man is taking good care of him," Pat said.

"Why didn't y'all stay with him?" Becky demanded.

Trent shook his head. "I wasn't allowed in the sweat lodge. And even though the Apaches are helping Bruce, they're none too friendly. Us hanging around might have caused an incident."

"Pat and Trent know what they're doing, Sis," Wes said as he walked up. "Let them handle things."

Becky suddenly rushed to Trent and buried her head against his chest.

As she sobbed, Trent wrapped his arms around her. "It'll be all right. You'll see. Your pa is a healthy man. He'll heal quick."

Becky lifted her head to look up at him. "I don't know what we would do without you and Pat."

Trent smiled. "You would be just fine. You have Wes and Pony Boy. Now, let's go into the house because I smell lamb stew. And I'm so hungry I could eat my socks."

For the next two days, Trent tried to keep busy cutting down and debarking trees for his cabin. However, Bruce wasn't far from his thoughts. Becky put on a good front to hide how worried she was, as did her mother. They busied themselves cleaning the cabin from top to bottom.

What time Trent wasn't cutting down pines, he visited the flock of sheep. There was something about watching Lobo and Pup work the sheep that relaxed him.

A cowboy in search of strays stumbled on Trent while he sat on a big rock with Pony Boy as they watched the sheep grazing in a meadow.

"Hey, what in the blazes are you doing running sheep on Mister McGregor's grazing range?" the man yelled.

Trent turned around slowly so he wouldn't spook the man into drawing his pistol. "This is Bruce Cowan's homestead. It's not Cord McGregor's range," Trent said. "Partner, you are trespassing."

"You best take your boy there and skedaddle before Mister McGregor burns you out. He'll never let you homestead this valley. He runs his cattle here in the winter. I'm here looking for strays."

"No one is burning us out. You can tell that to Cord," Trent said, using the rancher's first name as a sign of disrespect.

The cowboy nodded. "Pardner, I will tell him that. It's your funeral," the man added before whipping his horse around and galloping back the way he had come.

"I go after him?" Pony Boy asked.

Trent shook his head. "Nope, we can't do that," Trent said as he slipped off the rock and mounted Tex. "Keep up the outstanding work, Pony Boy," he called out before heading for the cabin.

Pat walked up as Trent released Tex in the corral. "You look worried."

"I just ran into one of Cord McGregor's cowboys out beating the bush for strays. He saw the sheep."

"That's not good. But it had to happen eventually. Now Cord has two reasons to run us out of the valley, homesteading and running sheep."

"Yup, I wonder which he hates more, sheep or homesteaders," Trent said.

"What do you plan on doing, Trent?"

Trent shook his head. "Nothing at the moment. We go back to the Apache camp tomorrow and fetch Bruce." Trent sighed. "I just hope he's in better condition than when we lift him."

"If not, we have to take him to the doctor in Salt Flats," Pat said

"Yup."

Chapter Eight
The Bear

"How are you feeling, Bruce?" Trent asked as they drove away from the Apache camp.

"Like I'll live. For a while, I was in doubt. I think I had a fever."

"Pat said you didn't have any swelling when he looked at your leg."

"Yeah, I don't know what they put on my leg, but it seemed to work. I'm still in some pain, but it's bearable now. What's been happening since I've been in the sweat lodge?"

"We found out that Owens's last name is McGill and there's a wanted poster on him," Pat called out from Leo as he rode alongside the wagon.

"That's good. It means Owens can't go to the sheriff and push his claim to your homestead, Trent."

"I didn't think of that angle. But we still have to deal with him. He will not want us settling so close to his hideout in the box canyon," Trent said.

"We aim on collecting the bounty on him, Bruce," Pat said

"You know how I feel about bounty hunters," Bruce reminded them.

"We know," Trent replied. "But, Bruce, it will come down to him or us."

Bruce didn't respond, so they were all quiet for a long moment.

"And one more thing. One of McGregor's cowboys discovered your flock of sheep while he was rounding up strays left in the valley during the roundup last year," Trent said.

"I didn't know we were hiding the sheep," Bruce said.

Trent ignored the remark. "McGregor will react like a wounded bear to the news of you running sheep."

"Let him. I ain't giving up my sheep, Trent."

"Yup, I know. I'm just telling you this because I suspect it might come to a shooting match."

"You know I'm a man of peace, Trent, but I ain't going to let another man tell me what I can and can't do on my land."

"I'm with you on that, Bruce," Pat said.

Trent sighed. "It will get ugly."

"We're getting close to home. Let's not bring our trouble into the house," Bruce said.

Wes, Becky, and Lois stood in front of the cabin a few minutes later when Trent pulled the wagon up. Becky and Lois rushed over to the side of the wagon.

"Pa, are you all right?" Becky asked.

"I'll be as good as new in two weeks," Bruce said.

"I missed you something terrible," Lois said as she reached into the wagon and touched her hand to Bruce's cheek. "Welcome home, honey."

Bruce smiled from ear to ear. "Yes, and I missed you too, dear."

"Look what I got you, Pa," Wes said as he held up a crude crutch."

"That's just what I need, son. Help me out of the back of the wagon, and I'll try it."

Trent and Pat hurried over to help Bruce to the edge of the wagon. Bruce put the V end of the crutch under his armpit and slid off the back of the wagon. He took two hesitant steps. "I'll get faster once I get the hang of using it."

Lois put her hand on her hips. "You need to get into the house and go to bed. You need rest, Bruce."

"Yeah, I reckon I do," Bruce said. His face looked pale.

Later, Trent, Pat, and Wes huddled together on a pine log near the site Trent had built his cabin.

"We have a lot of problems facing us," Trent said. "Trouble on every side."

"What's the most urgent threat?" Wes asked.

"McGregor sending men to drive our sheep away or kill them," Trent replied. "So far, he doesn't know we are the ones who have the homestead. If that were the case, he would ride here with a slew of men to burn us out."

"We have to post a lookout," Wes said and glanced at Pat Pat shook his head.

"If he sends men, they won't come at night, not with the Apaches in the area," Trent said.

"I must watch the trail coming from Salt Flats. There's a bluff near the river that gives a good view north across the prairie. I can spot riders miles away."

Trent nodded. "Good, take some supplies. You will have to make a camp on the bluff and keep a constant eye on the trail. At the first sign of dust, hightail it back here. We need time to put the sheep in the corral. We can protect them better there."

Pat nodded. "I'll leave at first light tomorrow morning."

"What about Owens McGill's gang?" Wes asked. "Pat said we will collect bounties on them."

Trent shook his head. "Not right away. I'm afraid if we go after the gang, McGregor's men will attack us."

"Trent, if we put some of McGregor's men in the dirt, it will be open war between them and us, sheepherder against cattlemen," Pat said. "It ain't going to be pretty."

"But my pa is within his rights to run sheep on his homestead," Wes said.

Trent sighed. "Wes, do you think for an instant the sheriff in Salt Flats will side with Bruce against Cord McGregor? Not on your life!"

"Na, I guess not," Wes replied.

"Ah, Wes," Trent said

"Yeah?"

"I met a preacher in the Cattleman's Saloon. And I asked him if he would marry Becky and me. Do you think Bruce will give his consent?" Trent asked.

Wes nodded as he smiled. "It will make him very happy, Trent."

"I haven't found the right moment to ask Becky, so keep it under your hat."

"Forty mules couldn't drag it from me."

"When do we raise your cabin?" Pat asked.

Trent shook his head. "With all the trouble going on, I'm reluctant to start. But I guess we could yoke the oxen and start hauling the logs up to the site tomorrow. Get everything in place, and then when it looks safe, raise the cabin."

Wes stood. "I'm going to the river to bathe and take a swim. Does anyone want to join me?"

"I will," Pat said eagerly.

Trent shook his head. "I want to check on Pony Boy and the flock. I haven't said hi to Lobo for a couple of days."

"Yeah, Trent, you lost your protector. He won't leave Pup's side. And I think she will have his pups soon."

That made Trent smile as he watched the two head for the river. He wondered if he had gone too far by telling Wes he planned to ask Becky to marry him. But he had wanted to see his reaction. If Bruce reacted as Wes predicted, Trent would do a jig.

He heard the bleating of the sheep and Pup barking as he approached the meadow. The trees were too large to use for building the cabin. That pleased Trent. He enjoyed walking among the towering trees.

Chapter Nine
A Boy in the Woods

Trent stumbled upon the boy's body as he walked back from the cabin for lunch. He had spent the morning trimming the logs and stripping off the bark. Someone had smashed in the top of the boys' head. The young Apache had been dead about a week, Trent guessed. Immediately, he concluded the McGregor's ranch hand that had stumbled onto Bruce's flock of sheep must have been the murderer.

Trent backtracked. He didn't want to disturb the ground around the body. He wanted Pat to look and try to track the killer. If his suspicions were correct, the trail would lead toward Salt Flats.

"What's your rush?" Bruce asked from his chair in front of the cabin.

"I discovered an Apache boy's body among the pines," Trent said.

"That's a shame. Who would kill a boy?" Bruce asked.

"The cavalry, for one," Trent said. "Sorry, I'm upset. However, it's true. The cavalry killed men, women, and children at the Sand Creek Massacre. They killed five hundred Cheyenne and Arapaho." Trent stopped and took a deep breath. "But I think the boy's killer is McGregor's ranch hand we caught near the sheep."

"That's a serious accusation. Are you sure it was McGregor's man?" Bruce asked.

"I will fetch Pat. He needs to have a look at the ground around the body to see if he can track the killer."

"He's out watching the trail from Salt Flats, right?"

"Yup, I don't want to be caught with my boots off in case McGregor sends some riders to burn us out."

Bruce shook his head. "All because we have a flock of sheep."

Trent shrugged. "Sheep threaten the way of life in these parts of Texas."

Bruce shook his head. "Yeah, you keep telling me that, but it's hard for me to swallow."

"I best fetch Pat," Trent said as he touched the brim of his hat before he continued toward the horse corral.

Trent rode Tex hard. He arrived at the bluff in less than an hour.

"I saw you coming a mile away," Pat said.

Trent shrugged. "I didn't hide."

"So what caused you to burn leather out here?"

Trent sighed. "Pat, I think the man we caught spying on the sheep killed an Apache boy I found in the woods. I need you to return with me and see if you can pick up the killer's tracks."

"It's been almost a week," Pat said.

"Yup. What do you think? Is there a chance to pick up the killer's trail?"

"In the pine forest?" Pat asked.

"Yup."

"Yeah, there's a good chance. The pine needles under the trees will hold a horseshoe imprint for days."

"Well, let's head back. I want to get the body to Chief Red Hawk as soon as possible."

"He ain't going to take it kindly that someone killed a boy," Pat said.

"Yeah, well, that's why we need to know who killed the boy before we take the body to the chief."

They stopped by and got Pony Boy to follow them to the body. Trent waited on Tex while Pat and Pony Boy searched the ground around the body. It took a while, but finally, Pony Boy found horse tracks leading away from the area.

The three followed the tracks, with Pony Boy walking between the two horses as he trailed the horse. Pony Boy's tracking ability surprised Trent. He had thought Pat an expert tracker, and he was. However, Pony Boy surpassed him.

The tracks led from the woods down to the river and then downriver. When the hoof prints merged with tracks left by Trent and Pat, even Pony Boy lost the trail.

"In my opinion," Trent said as they turned back. "It was the same man we confronted near the sheep."

Pat concurred. "Yup, I know."

"We kill many white men?" Pony Boy asked.

Trent shook his head. "Maybe the Apaches will, but not you. You're a shepherd. Protect the flock."

"Okay," Pony Boy said, sounding content to tend the sheep.

Trent and Pat rode back to the cabin to fetch the wagon. Bruce still sat in front of the cabin. Becky walked out of the cabin as Trent dismounted.

"Pa said someone killed a boy," Becky said. She sounded sad. "What a shame to snuff out the life of someone so young. Who would do such a thing, Trent?"

Trent paused and glanced over at Bruce before he answered. "A cowboy from one of the big ranches in the area who came to round up strays," Trent said carefully, not wanting to reveal McGregor's name but not wanting to lie either.

"I hope the Apaches make the rancher pay the price of killing the boy," Becky snapped.

"Yup, I have a hunch that Chief Red Hawk will make the rancher exact a heavy price for what his man did."

"He won't attack us, will he, Trent?" Becky asked with a hint of fear in her voice as she recalled the Comanche man who almost killed her during an attack on the wagons.

Trent shook his head. "Let's hope not. Pat and I will use the wagon to drive the boy back to the tribe."

Becky turned to her father. "Pa, you been outside long enough. You need to go to bed and get some rest."

"Trent be careful. Becky is a strong-willed woman," Bruce called out as he stood and used his crutch to walk to the door.

"Pa, what a thing to say to Trent!" Becky scolded her father as she followed him inside the cabin.

"You will be worse than hogtied, Trent," Pat joked as they hitched a team of horses to the wagon. He leaned forward.

"I see you already fear her wrath. You failed to mention McGregor by name."

Trent shook his head. "One battle at a time, Pat. Now stop jawing and finish hitching up the horses.

Pat raised his hands. "Hey, don't shoot the messenger."

"I'll fetch a horse blanket to wrap the body in while you finish up here," Trent said as he walked back to the lean-to at the far end of the horse corral.

A few minutes later, they were driving the wagon through the woods. Luckily, the pine needles kept the underbrush to a minimum among the pine forest. Wrapping the body fell to Trent since Pat, for reasons only known to him, refused to touch the dead boy's body until Trent wrapped it.

"I hope Red Hawk doesn't kill us for bringing him the boy," Trent said as Pat got the wagon underway.

"Red Hawk might not kill us, but he dang sure will hurt someone for killing the boy."

Two miles before they reached the hill beyond which the Apache village lay, two mounted braves carrying Winchesters suddenly appeared and mirrored their progress through the woods.

"I think McGregor has been giving them rifles," Pat said.

"If that's the case, he will regret it," Trent said. "Pat, make sure you tell the chief that one of McGregor's men killed the boy. We can't let him think we had anything to do with the boy's death."

A band of whooping Apaches charged the wagon as Pat drove up the hill. Neither man reacted to them. They swooped past the wagon and turned back to surround Trent and Pat. One broke away from the group and rode hard down the hill to the village.

"He's going to fetch Red Hawk. I think they know we've found their missing boy."

Red Hawk and two dozen older Apaches waited for the wagon in front of the chief's tipi.

Pat gave greetings to the chief in the Apache tongue. After that, Trent couldn't follow the conversation as Pat intertwined sign language while carrying on a verbal discussion with the chief. Throughout the conversation, Chief Red Hawk's facial expressions didn't alter. However, Trent knew the chief boiled with anger. His body grew tense and his words became louder.

When Pat finished, Chief Red Hawk barked orders to his men. Two rushed over to the wagon and lifted the boy wrapped in the horse blanket out of the wagon bed. They laid him at Chief Red Hawk's feet. Then, after the chief made a motion with his hand, the two men unrolled the horse blanket.

Several women in the group of onlookers wailed at the sight of the dead boy. One pulled her knife and started cutting her arm as she howled in grief. Chief Red Hawk spoke to the women, and four of them ran forward and lifted the body and carried it away. After they removed the body, the chief turned to Pat and spoke while making a motion that Trent interpreted as leave.

Pat immediately returned to the wagon and climbed into the seat. The Apaches cleared a path for Pat to turn the wagon. "For a moment, I thought Chief Red Hawk would have us killed," Pat said. "The boy is his grandson."

"That ain't good," Trent said.

"It sure ain't good for McGregor or any other settlers in the area," Pat agreed. "He said the land would run red with the white man's blood."

"Pat, you know that, in the long run, it will go bad for the Apaches. If they attack the settlers or ranchers, the cavalry will swoop down on the village and massacre the entire tribe like they did at Sand Creek."

"Yup, but what can we do? If we try to interfere, Red Hawk will attack the cabin and kill us all," Pat said.

Trent shrugged. "It ties our hands. And there's no guarantee some of Red Hawk's men won't disobey his orders and attack us."

"We have to keep vigilant," Pat agreed.

Trent shook his head. "Now we're stuck between three enemies, Owens McGill, Cord McGregor, and Chief Red Hawk. And we are only five men to stand up against them."

"Yup, but five men who can shoot center," Pat reminded Trent. "We've faced worse odds before," he added.

Trent shook his head. "I'm not thinking about us, Pat. It's Bruce and the women who are on my mind. No matter what happens, I want Wes to remain at the cabin in case of trouble. He must protect his family when we're away."

"Where are we going?" Pat asked.

"You're going back to the bluff to watch the coming and going on the plains. I think you'll see a lot of activity."

"Yeah, if McGregor sends men against us, he will run into a hornet's nest of angry Apaches," Pat said.

Wes ran up to the wagon as Pat pulled into the yard. "At least you didn't lose your hair."

"The tribe would have retaliated if it hadn't been for Chief Red Hawk. But he looked as though he wanted to as well."

"Are we safe from an attack?" Bruce called out from his chair in front of the door.

"For now. But the situation could change. We have to stock up the cabin in case we have to shelter in it during an attack," Trent said.

"But what about the sheep?" Bruce asked.

"We'll have Pony Boy keep them close to the cabin. If we get wind of an attack, we'll drive them into the corral. We can defend the corral from the cabin during an attack," Trent said.

Bruce shook his head. "Let's hope it doesn't come to that."

Chapter Ten
A Hornet's Nest

"It's been four days," Bruce said as he hobbled out the door to greet Trent. "Maybe cooler heads have prevailed among the Apache."

Trent dropped Tex's reins and walked over as Bruce took a seat in his chair. He shook his head. "I doubt it. If there's one thing I have learned about the Apaches is that they are patient. Chief Red Hawk will get his revenge when he sees an opportunity."

"At least they haven't bothered us none."

"They have lookouts watching us, Bruce. Pat spotted two yesterday in the woods near the cabin on his way to the bluff," Trent said.

"Do you think they are planning an attack?"

Trent shook his head, "Nope, they are just making sure we aren't in cahoots with McGregor."

"So we don't have to worry about an attack?" Bruce asked.

"Yup, at least not at the moment." Trent nodded toward the flock of sheep. "I see Pony Boy is keeping the flock close to the cabin."

"Yeah, and I must admit I enjoy watching Lobo and Pup work the sheep. It's more entertaining than a square dance."

Trent nodded. "I hardly ever see Lobo anymore."

"I don't think Pony Boy could manage the sheep without him and Pup."

Trent started to speak when Pat galloped up to the cabin with Leo all lathered up.

"Riders are coming from Salt Flats, about thirty," Pat called out as he remained mounted.

Wes rushed out of the house. "Is it McGregor's men?"

Pat nodded. "More than likely. But he ain't going to make it to the cabin. I spotted an Apache scout burning leather toward the village. If I was a betting man, I would say Red Hawk will ambush the men when they enter the woods along the river."

"Trent," Bruce called out. "What are we going to do?"

Trent shook his head. "Nothing but wait and see what happens. If we warn McGregor's men, it ain't going to change his mind about us running sheep on his grazing land. He'll take on the Apaches and then us."

"Yeah, I know. But I hate to see McGregor's men ride into an ambush."

"One of them killed Chief Red Hawk's grandson. They have to answer for that, Bruce. The law ain't going to do anything to the man who killed an Apache boy."

"Yeah, I hear you," Bruce said and then fell silent.

"If the Apaches attack McGregor's men and win, it'll keep McGregor out of your hair for a while. He'll be too busy fighting Apaches to worry about a flock of sheep. And Red Hawk will have his hands full with McGregor." Trent said.

"I agree with Trent," Pat said. "We watch but don't interfere. We let the chips fall where they will."

Wes nodded. "Pa, they're right."

Bruce sighed. "Yeah, I know they're right, but I'm a peace-loving man, and I don't like it one bit."

"Wes, you stay and look after your folks. I'm going back to the bluff to watch what happens. If the Apaches don't attack McGregor's men, Pat and I will have to confront them."

"Trent, if you kill some of McGregor's men, you will be branded an outlaw," Bruce warned.

"Yup, but then I can't let them burn the cabin and kill the sheep, can I Bruce?"

Bruce shook his head. "No, son. You can't."

"Come on, Pat. I'll saddle Tex," Trent said as he headed for the corral."

"Trent, we're between the fire and the frying pan," Pat said.

"Yup. We might have to do something that'll make us wanted men, Pat. But I'll be danged if I'll let McGregor's men drive Bruce off his homestead."

"Okay, I'm with you," Pat said as he watched Trent saddle Tex. "But where do we go?"

"You know that group of boulders on the riverbank about halfway between the cabin and the bluff?"

"Yup."

"I reckon I'll set up there with my Sharps. You hide among the trees. If McGregor's men make it to that point, you step out and confront them while I cover you from the rocks. If they are set on a confrontation, I'll start sending them to boot hill."

"The law will see it as murder, Trent."

"I know, Pat. But they ain't going to get past us."

"Okay, I guess we have to protect the Cowans. That's kind of what we hired on to do," Pat said.

"Yup, we did, and the job ain't over."

The two brothers didn't speak again until they reached the rock formation on the bank of the Canadian River.

"This is the spot, Pat. I'll tie Tex out of sight and climb up to the top. You ride over to the pines on the other side of the trail and wait. I'll whistle when I want you to confront the riders."

Pat turned Leo to the left. "Okay," he called over his shoulder.

"Good luck, Pat, and shoot center."

"You too, brother," Pat called over his shoulder.

For one of the few times in his life, Trent found himself nervous. The thought of gunplay didn't bother him. The notion that he might never see Becky again did. He had many words built up inside of him he wanted to tell her but had never found the courage to speak. The thought of getting cut down by a bullet and leaving all those things unsaid made him as nervous as a long-tailed cat on a porch of rocking chairs.

He shoved all thoughts of Becky from his mind. He needed to be calm, to shoot center. And if the Apaches didn't stop McGregor's men, he would have to do a lot of shooting. He pulled cartridges out of his gun belt and laid them in a row on the boulder beside his buffalo rifle.

Now he had to wait.

Trent listened for the sound of horses. He heard a blue jay scolding a fox from the safety of a pine tree and squirrels chattering as they raced up and down an oak near the boulders. What he didn't hear was the sound of horses.

Time seemed to stand still as Trent listened to the sounds of the woods. The blue jay kept screaming as it fluttered from bush to bush while it followed the fox. The squirrels sensed the nearness of the fox and scampered up into the oak.

When the jay suddenly fell silent, Trent paid attention. He listened but didn't hear a sound. The entire area had suddenly gone quiet. He peered down the trail. Nothing! But something was afoot, Trent felt sure of that. What? He didn't hear horses.

Trent glanced at the pine thicket Pat had disappeared into. Maybe his brother had dismounted and crept closer to the trail and had spooked the bird.

Then he heard it—the sound of horses. Still far off, but heading toward him. "Dang it. I was hoping the Apaches had made quick work of McGregor's men," Trent muttered under his breath. It would have solved the McGregor problem, at least for the time being.

From the sound of the horses, Trent knew the men had slowed their mounts to a walk. He aimed downriver and waited. The first riders appeared a few moments later. They rode four abreast like a troop of cavalry. Each held a Winchester in his right hand, pointed skyward.

"Hmm, they mean business," Trent whispered while he watched the horsemen ride closer and closer. "When do I signal, Pat?" Trent mumbled. He knew the moment Pat stepped out in the open, McGregor's men would try to shoot him dead. However, he couldn't let them burn the cabin and kill the Cowan family.

I'll try to shoot the first four riders if it looks as though they will open fire on Pat, Trent told himself. And Pat is resourceful. He's not just going to stand tall and let them gun him down.

Trent put two fingers in his mouth and whistled when he heard a whooshing sound. A flight of arrows impaled the chests of the first four riders. The riders behind the first men knew nothing was amiss until they fell off their horses.

"Apaches! We are under attack!" one of the mounted men shouted as flight after flight of arrows filled the air from the ground and trees. "Some of them are in the trees!" the same fellow shouted just before he took an arrow in the stomach and pitched forward off his horse.

The mounted men started firing into the brush and the canopy of the trees. Arrows gave way to rifles as the Apaches dropped their bows and fired their Winchesters.

Trent made a quick decision and whistled for Pat just before he shot one of McGregor's men off his horse. Pat, knowing what Trent wanted him to do, opened fire with both pistols from his hiding place. Men dropped like flies. When they suddenly lost half their members, it spooked the riders. One near the rear of the column turned his horse and fled. Other riders spotted the man galloping away and joined him. In a matter of moments, McGregor's men were in full retreat.

"I bet they don't stop until they get back to Salt Flats," Trent said as he stood. He expected the Apaches to show themselves, but none stepped into view. Only Pat emerged from behind a ponderosa and waved his pistols at Trent. The Apaches had melted into the forest.

Pat met Trent when he climbed off the boulder. "For a moment, I thought I wouldn't see another sunrise," Pat said. "I figured the moment I stepped out from behind that pine, they would open fire on me."

"Yep, I had the same thought, Pat. The Apaches saved our bacon."

"Well, mine at least," Pat said. "It sorts of balances the scale with Apaches killing Ma and Pa."

"Yup, it does. Not that these Apaches had any involvement in their death," Trent said.

"Trent, I'm not sure the Apaches would have won the battle if we hadn't thrown our support to them. These men seemed rather disciplined for ranch hands. It's almost like someone has been drilling them in cavalry tactics."

"They showed their inexperience. If McGregor's men had been U.S. troops, they would have dismounted and taken firing positions when the Apaches killed the first riders."

"I, for one, am glad they weren't professional soldiers," Pat said.

"Pat, you know and I do that the next opponents the Apaches will face is a company of U.S. Cavalry. Now that Chief Red Hawk has broken the treaty, they will send troops from Fort Dodge to subdue him."

Pat nodded. "Yup, and our hands are tied. We can't let the Cowans know we fought alongside the Apaches. Bruce wouldn't like it we killed some of McGregor's men. He's still ain't adjusted to the rules of the frontier. Part of him is still in Boston."

"We will tell Bruce the Apaches attacked McGregor's men before we had a chance to jaw with them. And since it wasn't our fight, we didn't take sides."

"Yeah, that sounds believable," Pat said.

"I don't like lying, Pat, but sometimes one has to stretch the truth."

Chapter Eleven
A Trip to Salt Flats

Everyone except Pony Boy stood waiting for Trent and Pat in front of the cabin. Becky charged forward to walk alongside Tex. "What was all the shooting about, Trent? Are you hurt?"

Trent smiled down at Becky. "I'm fine. The Apaches attacked McGregor's men and sent them packing. I'm sure they didn't slow down until they got to Salt Flats."

"I thought I heard a buffalo rifle," Bruce said.

"The Apaches had one," Pat lied to keep his brother from having to do so.

Bruce shook his head. "I see."

"We need the wagon, Bruce." Trent said after he dismounted.

"What for?" Bruce asked.

"We need to gather up the bodies and take them to Salt Flats. It wouldn't be right to leave them for the varmints," Trent replied.

"You ain't going to be welcome in town," Wes said.

"That can't be helped. We have to get the bodies to Salt Flats for a proper burial," Trent said.

"Maybe Sheriff Givens will think you killed them," Wes said.

"A lot of the bodies have arrows. And McGregor knows the Apaches have Winchesters since he gave the rifles to them," Pat said.

"Trent, is McGregor in Salt Flats?" Becky demanded.

Trent gave Pat a hard look. His brother shrugged. "Yeah, his spread runs from just north of the Canadian to Salt Flats," Trent said.

"That sounds like an enormous ranch," Becky said.

"Yup, the biggest one in the panhandle of Texas," Pat said.

"Trent, if McGregor is in Salt Flats, I don't like you going to town. He stampeded his cattle to kill us all," Becky reminded Trent.

"Yup, he did. But we're still here. I ain't afraid of McGregor. And we have to take the bodies to town, Becky. We have to."

"Will one wagon hold all the bodies?" Pat asked.

"Yup, but we'll need a team of four horses. It'll be too heavy for just two."

"I'll hitch the horses to the wagon," Pat said. He nodded at Wes. "Come on and help."

"Trent, how long have you known McGregor had his ranch near Salt Flats?"

"I didn't want you to worry about me, Becky," Trent said.

Becky glanced over at her father. "I guess you knew all along, Pa?"

"It's the men's job to worry, not the women's," Bruce said as he looked at his wife as he spoke.

Lois nodded her head. "He's right, Becky. If we had known McGregor had his spread nearby, we would have worried ourselves sick."

Becky ignored her mother's comments. "Trent, is he going to drive us off our homestead?"

"Yup, he will try."

"Why?"

Trent glanced at Bruce and then sighed before he looked at Becky. "Two reasons... well, three. First, he hates Pat and me 'cause we are part Yaqui. Second, he grazes his cattle in Broad Valley and don't want homesteaders constructing fences that will cut his cattle off from prime grazing grass. And last but not least are your father's sheep. Cattlemen hate sheep. They say sheep overgraze the land."

Becky looked shocked at what Trent had said. "If the sheep are a problem, then the problem isn't just with McGregor but all the ranchers in the area."

"Yup," Trent said.

"Pa, how are we going to deal with everyone against us? Maybe we should pull up stakes and head to California."

Bruce shook his head vigorously. "Becky, I'm never moving from this homestead. And I will not let anyone tell me what I can and can't do on my property. I'll fight for this land with my last breath."

Becky, her face pale, glanced at Trent.

"A man's got to fight for what he believes in or he ain't a man," Trent said.

Becky stiffened her back as she pursed her lips. "You just better not get yourself killed, Trent. You hear me!"

Trent nodded and smiled. "Loud and clear, Becky. Don't worry, I will be around for a long time. I ain't that easy to get rid of."

The sound of a wagon signaled that Pat had finished hitching up the horses and was ready to go pick up the bodies. Wes rode behind the wagon on his Quarter Horse to help.

Trent tipped his hat at Becky. "I've got to go. We need to return the dead men to Salt Flats so they get a proper funeral," Trent said.

Becky shook her fingers at Trent. "You better be careful, Trent McLcod!

"Yup, roped and hogtied," Pat whispered as Trent climbed into the wagon.

"Stop flapping your lip and drive," Trent said with a big smile on his face.

Wes shook his head when they got to the site, and he looked at the first couple of men lying in front of his horse. "I wish I hadn't volunteered for this."

"Yup," Trent said as he climbed down from the wagon.

"Pat, aren't you going to help load them?" Wes asked.

"Nope, it's women's work to tend the dead," Pat replied.

Wes glanced at Trent.

Trent shrugged but didn't comment.

"But what if I hadn't of come with y'all?" Wes asked.

"But you did. Now grab this one's feet," Trent said.

When they finished, Wes shook his head. "Dang it, I hope I never have to do this again."

"Okay, you need to get back to the cabin, Wes," Trent said.

"Yeah, and I will take a swim in the river. I feel unclean after handling all those bodies."

"Stick close to the cabin and be on the lookout for both Apaches and Owenses men. I don't think we have to worry about any of McGregor's men for a time," Trent said as he watched Wes mount his horse.

"I'll keep your sweetheart safe, Trent," Wes teased.

Trent tried to hide his smile while he watched Wes ride away.

"Trent, I'm not worried about the Apaches attacking the cabin. Chief Red Hawk knows we helped in the battle."

"Yup, but there is still Owens. Eventually, we need to eliminate that problem."

Pat nodded while he slapped the reins against the back of the horses. "I suppose we do."

"Getting out of Salt Flats alive will not be as easy as picking blueberries," Trent said a little later when the wagon turned away from the Canadian River and headed across the prairie.

"The grass doesn't grow well in these parts as we've seen it grow along the Santa Fe Trail, yet everyone wants to settle in Texas," Pat said.

"I think settling in Texas is a romantic notion in the east," Trent replied. "But then I can't blame them. Texas gets in your blood. It's home for me."

"Wherever I place my bedroll at night is home to me," Pat said.

"You'll find a woman one of these days and raise a home full of babies," Trent teased.

Pat made a snorting sound.

"It could happen. That sand might shift out of your boots one of these days," Trent said.

Ignoring his remark, Pat asked, "Do I circle and drive in from the north?"

Trent shook his head. "Nope, they realize now we have a homestead along the Canadian River."

Pat nodded. "Yup, that's what I figure too."

As the wagon rolled into Salt Flats, Trent glanced down the long road that ran through the town. At the far end, he could see the steeple of the church that only welcomed ranchers. Trent made a note to visit Preacher Jetson's adobe church, where he hoped one day soon to marry Becky.

"Where to now?" Pat asked.

"Sheriff Givens's office," Trent said.

Sheriff Givens must have seen the wagon stop in front of the jail because he hurried outside.

"You two have some huevos riding into town!" he exclaimed in a voice that carried a distance. "What do y'all got in the wagon?"

"Chief Red Hawk attacked the men Cord McGregor sent to burn us out!" Trent replied. "We gathered up the dead and hauled them here for a proper burial. It seemed the Christian thing to do."

Sheriff Givens shook his head. "I know nothing about him sending men to burn you out!"

"Yup," Pat said. "I'm sure you don't, Sheriff. It's called looking the other way."

Trent could see Sheriff Givens's jaw working as he ground his teeth before he answered. "Are you saying I'm shirking my duties as sheriff of Salt Flats?"

"Yup, but that's kind of sugarcoating it, don't you think, Pat?" Trent said as he glanced across the seat at Pat.

"Sugarcoating a cow patty if you ask me," Pat said. "You're in Cord McGregor's pocket is what I believe."

Sheriff Givens's face turned bright red. He squared himself to Pat as though he meant to draw his pistol.

"Sheriff, if your hand touches the grip of your pistol, you're heading to boot hill," Pat said calmly.

"Are you threatening me, boy?"

"It ain't a threat unless you touch your pistol. Then it'll be a fact," Pat replied.

"Sheriff, which way is the undertaker? We need to unload the bodies and leave. We didn't come into Salt Flats looking for trouble. Just to do the Christian thing."

"Let me have a look in the wagon," Sheriff Givens demanded as he walked toward them.

"Have at it," Pat said.

Sheriff Givens glanced angrily at Pat but didn't speak as he walked to the back of the wagon. "Lord God!" Sheriff Givens shrieked. A few moments later, he walked back to the front of the wagon. "I saw arrows, but I also saw sizeable holes that only a buffalo rifle could make," Sheriff Givens said in an accusing tone while staring at Trent's Sharps.

"One of the Apaches had a Remington Rolling Block rifle," Pat lied.

"Oh, I wonder where they got it?" Sheriff Givens asked.

"Maybe you should ask that question to Cord McGregor," Trent said. "Now, if you will kindly direct us to the undertaker, we'll be on our way."

"That went about as well as expected," Trent said an hour later as Pat drove out of town.

"Yup, we surely dodged the bullet. We didn't run into McGregor or any of his men," Trent said.

"I sort of hoped that this Red fellow would arrive and confront us while we were in town. I've got a hankering to see just how fast he can draw his pistol, Trent. I got to know."

"Pat, don't push your luck. I ain't seen him draw his Colt, but he has the quickness of a cat in the way he moves. I'm guessing he's mighty fast on the draw."

"So you say, Trent. So you say."

"Pat, head east when we leave town. I want to pay a visit to Preacher Jetson's church," Trent said.

"What? Do you hear wedding bells in your head, Trent?"

"No! I just want to check out the church. I certainly ain't going to get married in a pigsty."

Pat smiled and raised his hands in surrender.

The whitewashed adobe building sat on the prairie a mile from town. The church's stark surroundings gave the building an insignificant look, as though it were an afterthought.

Pat shook his head, "I hope it looks better on the inside."

"I'm not looking for fancy, Pat."

"Good, 'cause it doesn't come close to fancy," Pat said as he stopped the wagon in front of the building.

Trent climbed down from the wagon when the sound of galloping horses caught his attention. He glanced behind the wagon. "We got trouble coming, Pat."

Pat turned to look. "They're carrying torches and a bucket of tar," Pat said after he shaded his eyes to stare at the horseman.

Trent shook his head. "They mean to burn the church."

"So much for getting out of Salt Flats without getting in trouble," Pat said.

"Pat, don't kill anyone!" Trent said in a stern voice.

"Dang, it's got to where a man can't have any fun anymore," Pat said.

"Pat!" Trent said, raising his voice.

"Okay, no killing," Pat said.

Trent rolled his eyes. "Sometimes, I think the doctor slapped your head instead of your butt when you were born, Pat." Trent sighed as he climbed down from the wagon. He took a stance in front of the church's door.

"What's going on?" Preacher Jetson said as he emerged from the church in a dirty shirt and jeans. When he saw the shocked look on Trent's face, he added, "Well, Trent, I told you I drank during the week."

"Yup, you did. Now get back inside while Pat and I handle the situation," Trent said as he grabbed the preacher and turned him around.

"What situation?" Preacher Jetson said as he resisted efforts to propel him toward the church door.

"That Jeremiah fellow I confronted in the saloon is coming to burn the church," Trent said as he recognized the leading rider.

"God must have sent you to save the church!" Preacher Jetson exclaimed. "Praise the Lord."

"Trent, get him inside. The sight of him liquored up will just entice them farther," Pat said. "I'll handle the mob," he said as he hopped down from the wagon seat.

He took several steps away from the wagon and squared himself to the approaching riders. One horse reared back as it stopped, but the rider got it under control.

"Howdy, folks," Pat said, emphasizing his Texas accent. "What can I do for you?"

"Get out of our way," Jeremiah said as he waved the torch back and forth. "We will burn this heathen church to the ground."

"I'm afraid I can't allow that. My brother plans on getting married in this church," Pat said.

"Yeah, well, he will have to find another place to get hitched," Jeremiah said.

Pat shook his head. "No, that's not what will happen. You will drop the torches and that bucket of tar. Then you and your men will turn tail and ride back to the rat holes you crawled out of."

"Them's mighty strong words. Maybe you don't have no schooling and can't count. There's six of us and only one of you," Jeremiah said as he glanced at his friends and chuckled.

"I'm packing two Colts. That's twelve bullets, but only six men. I guess I'll just have to use one pistol," Pat said.

Jeremiah noticed Pat's double holster for the first time. He cleared his throat. "You can't be that good."

Pat drew and fired. The bullet snapped the torch Jeremiah held in half. As quickly as he had drawn his pistol,

Pat twirled it back into his holster. "I'm sorry. I didn't catch what you said, pardner," Pat said. "Could you say again?"

"Jeremiah, I think I'll head on back to the saloon," one rider said before turning his horse around and yelling, "Giddyup!"

Pat placed both hands on his pistols. "Get!" he shouted.

Jeremiah hesitated a moment before he whipped his horse around and rode after his friends.

"I heard a shot. Did you kill someone, Pat?" Trent asked as he walked out of the church.

"Nope, I just killed a torch."

Chapter Twelve
The Cavalry

Wes walked up to stand beside Trent. "It's a pretty sight," he said as he looked at the cabin.

"Beautiful," Trent replied.

Three weeks of backbreaking work had gone into raising Trent's cabin. The door faced the south and had a view of the river and the valley.

"Thanks for all the hard work, Wes," Trent said. "I really appreciate it."

"Got to see that Sis has a suitable home!" Wes replied. "When are you going to pop the question?"

"When the time is right. It ain't now. We have several dark clouds hanging over us. I will not marry Becky just to make her a widow."

"Yeah, trouble is brewing on all sides. The Apaches are on the warpath, burning and looting the ranches east along the river. Then we have Owens and his gang. But since the Apache uprising, they haven't ventured out of their canyon much."

Trent nodded. "I think the least of our worries is Cord McGregor. He ain't recovered from the Apaches' attack on his men."

"Yeah, I reckon his men will not be easily persuaded to return to Broad Valley after their run-in with Chief Red Hawk," Wes agreed. "So what problem are you planning on taking on first?"

"I have a mind to collect the bounty on Owens and his men. I'm afraid that once the Apaches calm down, he will bushwhack us and take the cabins for himself."

"I just don't see how he can hope to hold on to the homestead since he's a wanted man," Wes said.

"He can use a different name or have one of his men register the homestead claim. There are ways," Trent said as he saw Bruce walking toward them. "Your father's leg is healed, but I'm afraid he'll always have a limp."

Bruce made his way to where the two stood. "Admiring your cabin, are you Trent?" he asked.

"You're doggone right I am. And I can't thank you enough for building the chimney," Trent said. Hearing a galloping horse, Trent looked beyond Bruce to see Pat riding Leo hard toward them.

Bruce turned and shook his head. "What now?"

Trent shrugged as he waited for Pat to rein Leo to a stop. "What's the matter, Pat?"

"A company of cavalry is heading toward the river!" Pat shouted.

"Pat, ride to the Apaches and warn them! I don't want to see another Sand Creek massacre!"

"What are you going to do?" Pat asked.

"I will slow them down and give Chief Red Hawk time to escape."

"What if he fights?" Pat asked.

"You persuade him otherwise. Tell him if he stays, the soldiers will kill women and children. Now get!"

Bruce looked shocked. "Trent, you can't kill soldiers!"

"I won't. I'm just going to keep them pinned down for a while," Trent said before he turned and ran over to Tex. He vaulted onto the palomino.

"Trent, do you want me to ride along?" Wes shouted.

"No, stay here," Trent called over his shoulder as he urged Tex into a full sprint.

Trent rode hard. He reached the cliff overlooking the prairie while the troops were still about a thousand yards from the river trail. Not wasting any time, he lay in a prone position and aimed his Sharps. Trent felt the kick against his shoulder and, a moment later, saw the hat fly off the leading trooper's head.

The troopers milled around until Trent shot a boulder nearby to show he meant business. The officer in charge must have given the order to dismount and take cover. As the troopers dismounted, Trent hoped the officer thought an attack was imminent.

After Trent spotted the officer in charge, he fired. The bullet hit its mark, another nearby rock. "I could just as easily have put you in the dirt," Trent mumbled.

As Trent kept up the fire, one trooper mounted his horse, only to have the animal rear back and dump its rider when a bullet hit the dirt right in front of it. After that, the soldiers hunkered down behind their mounts.

Trent continued to keep the troopers pinned down for another half hour. The officer finally figured out they were facing only one rifle and ordered his men to mount and charge Trent's position.

Hoping he had given the Apaches enough time to leave their village, Trent galloped Tex toward home. A mile away from the cabin, a group of Apache warriors charged out of the trees and surrounded Trent. Their leader recognized Trent and spoke quickly to his fellow Apaches.

The men let Trent pass and followed him. Near the cabin, Trent caught up with the women and children plodding along the riverbank. Travois carried the skins and poles used to construct their tipis, along with food and supplies. Trent marveled at how quickly the Apaches had dismantled their village.

Pat rode to meet Trent.

"Red Hawk sure put a fire under his people," Trent said.

Pat shook his head. "They had to leave a lot of the tipis and most of their belongings."

"That's too bad, but if they had stayed, you know what would have happened, Pat."

"Yup, and I convinced Chief Red Hawk. Some Apaches wanted to stay and fight. But they listened to Red Hawk."

"What are those women doing with the pine branches? Are they brushing away their tracks?" Trent asked.

Pat nodded. "Yup, the cavalry will search the valley for them when they find the village abandoned."

"They are moving fast," Trent said. "Do you know where they are headed?"

"Upriver to the Territory of New Mexico."

When Trent reached Bruce's cabin, he found everyone but Pony Boy standing in front, watching the Apaches marching past.

"Trent, you and Pat saved a lot of lives today. I'm proud of both of you. I just hope you didn't kill any soldiers," Bruce said.

"Nope, I came close though," Trent said.

The group stood in silence until the last of the Apaches disappeared down the river trail.

"You all come on inside. I've got vittles ready," Lois said.

"You don't have to ask me twice, Mama," Wes called out as he headed for the door.

"Trent, I'm proud of you too," Becky said as she held back to walk beside Trent.

"I always try to do the right thing, Becky. But, dang it, sometimes it's hard to figure out what's right and what's wrong."

"Trent, you seem to do a good job of figuring it out," Becky said as they entered the cabin.

"How does Pony Boy like sleeping in your cabin, Trent?" Bruce asked as they sat at the table.

Trent shook his head. "He still sleeps in the wagon near the flock in case bears or mountain lions attack the sheep. He says Lobo and Pup might get hurt defending the flock against big predators."

"When are Pup's puppies due?" Becky asked. "I love puppies. We need two dogs around the cabin..."

Trent held up his hand for silence. "I hear horses, lots of horses," he said as he jumped up and grabbed his Sharps. He hurried out the door, with Pat and Wes close behind.

"Hold up!" a loud voice called out as riders dressed in blue army uniforms trotted out of the woods on the east side of the cabin.

"The cavalry," Wes said.

"Lois, you and Becky stay in the house," Bruce said before he emerged from the door.

Trent, with his Sharps cradled in the crook of his arm, stepped forward to meet the troopers. "Howdy," he called out as a captain rode forward with a lieutenant to meet Trent. "What can I do for y'all?" Trent asked.

"We're searching for Apaches. Have you seen any? My scout said they were heading in this direction," the lieutenant said.

"Yup, I saw some a little while ago. I was up in the woods hunting deer. Saw a large group heading for the canyons. Why are they on the move?" Trent asked.

The lieutenant didn't answer, but the captain did. "Someone fired at us as we approached the river. They had a buffalo rifle. That's one you're carrying, isn't it?"

"The Apaches have a Remington Rolling Block .50 caliber rifle. I've seen them using it hunting mule deer," Pat spoke up.

"Remington? Where did they get such a fancy rifle?" the captain asked.

Bruce stepped next to Trent. "I heard a rancher named Cord McGregor has been giving them weapons, hoping they'll drive us, homesteaders, from the Canadian River valley."

"Yup," Trent said. "I heard that in Salt Flats too."

"This Mister McGregor would arm the Apaches?" the captain said in disbelief.

Trent shrugged. "Well, that's what folks in Salt Flats are claiming. I can't say how true it is, but when my brother and I gathered the men the Apaches killed in the battle with Cord's men, most died from bullet wounds."

"You say the Apaches headed toward the canyons?" the captain asked.

Trent nodded. "Yup."

The lieutenant pointed at Pat. "Captain, he's an Indian. Maybe they are lying to protect the tribe."

"Pat is my brother. We are both half Yaqui. We don't have any love for the Apaches. They killed our ma and pa."

"Did they now?" the captain said.

"Yup," Pat said.

The captain stared at Pat for a long moment. "Lieutenant, bring the troops. Let's go and check this out."

"Good luck," Bruce called out as the troopers filed past.

When the soldiers were out of sight, Trent turned to Bruce. "That should give Red Hawk enough time."

Bruce nodded. "Let's hope it does." He motioned toward the cabin. "Come on, and let's finish our meal."

"Pa, I was afraid the soldiers were going to arrest you all," Becky said as the men took seats at the table.

"I heard everything," Lois said. "Did they believe you, Trent?"

Trent shrugged. "I'm not sure, Miss Lois. But at least they headed for the canyons. That'll buy Chief Red Hawk some time. But I figure that, sooner or later, their scouts are going to pick up the Apaches' trail."

"It ain't going to be good for the soldiers if they do catch up with the Apaches," Pat said. "Chief Red Hawk will set up ambushes and pick off the soldiers a few at a time until they turn tail and head back to Fort Dodge."

Becky shook her head. "So much killing. When is it going to end?"

"Soon, Becky, real soon," Trent said determinedly.

Chapter Thirteen
The Bounty

Trent looked down at the river and the valley beyond from the door of his cabin. He and Pat had been sleeping on burlap bags of leaves. He hadn't had time to bang together two beds from split pine logs. Still, sleeping on the sacks of leaves was better than the ground.

Trent had it in his mind to split logs and build a floor before he asked Becky to marry him and move into the cabin. Bruce had used deer hides to cover the floor in his cabin. However, Trent wanted the wood floor even though it would take a lot of hard work to split the logs into planks.

Pistol shots suddenly echoed from the woods upriver. Trent grabbed his rifle and sprinted toward the shots. As he emerged from a stand of pines, he found Pony Boy lying on the ground, moaning. Next to the Arapaho lay two dead lambs with bullet wounds.

"What happened?" Trent shouted as he knelt beside Pony Boy.

"The outlaw, Owens. He and several men surrounded me. I couldn't draw my pistol. I had lambs in my arms. Would have killed me, but lambs took bullets meant for me. Caught one in shoulder. But Pony Boy play dead. They ride away."

"Let me have a look at your shoulder," Trent said as he unbuttoned the man's plaid shirt. "The bullet went clean through. Didn't hit a bone. You will be fine. Let me help you up and get you to the Cowans' cabin. Miss Lois can doctor you," Trent said as he helped Pony Boy to stand.

Becky must have seen Trent and Pony Boy through the window. She ran out of the cabin and rushed to meet them. "What happened?" Becky demanded.

"Owens shot Pony Boy. I guess it's another warning for us to leave the valley," Trent said while they walked Pony Boy to the cabin.

Becky shook her head. "We ain't leaving our homesteads, Trent!"

Becky's declaration caught Trent by surprise. He glanced at her as they helped Pony Boy into the cabin. "Put him in the chair at the head of the table," Trent called.

"What's wrong with Pony Boy?" Bruce asked as he rushed in from working the garden at the side of the cabin. He had planted onions and squash before they raised the cabin.

"Owens shot him. He killed two lambs. I'll go and fetch them before a coyote finds them. Where's Pat and Wes?"

"In the river washing up," Becky answered.

"Okay, I'll saddle Tex and stop by to tell them to get back to the cabin. Owens might return," Trent said. He tipped his hat. "Take good care of Pony Boy, Becky."

"Mama will sew him up if it needs stitches," Becky called out as Trent headed for the door.

"Dadburn it. I should have taken care of Owens sooner," Trent mumbled as he saddled Tex.

He found Pat and Wes splashing in the water like young children. As he dismounted, Trent reminded himself they were still boys in age, at least, but not in experience. "Grab your clothes," Trent shouted when he walked to the edge of the riverbank. "Owens shot Pony Boy."

"Is he dead?" Wes asked as he waded toward the bank.

"No, just got winged. Your sister is patching him up at the cabin. I've got to get the two lambs Owens killed. I'll meet you two at the cabin."

"Owens didn't kill Lobo or Pup, did he?" Pat asked.

"No, he stumbled onto Pony Boy returning two lambs to the flock."

"That's good," Wes said. "It would be hard to handle the sheep without the dogs."

"Yup," Trent said as he swung Tex around and trotted off toward the spot where he had found Pony Boy. He dismounted to study the ground around the two dead lambs. Trent shook his head. Owens had more men than the last time he ran into him. He had to do something before the gang grew so big he and Pat couldn't deal with them.

Trent tied the lambs' hinds legs and put them across the back of his saddle. Before he returned to the cabin, he headed for the flock. Trent heard Pup yelping before he spotted the sheep. When Lobo saw Trent, he raced up and leaped into the air.

"Yeah, I'm glad to see you too, Lobo," Trent said. He waited for the wolf-dog to calm down before he turned and headed back to the cabin. Lobo followed him a little way before Pup barked, and he turned to race back to the flock.

Pat and Wes had saddled their horses and waited beside them for Trent. Trent nodded to the two men as he dismounted and walked into the cabin. "How is he?" he asked Lois while she finished putting a bandage around Pony Boy's shoulder.

"He will be okay. I put honey on his bandages. The Apaches used it on Bruce's leg, and it didn't get infected."

"Trent, I see that Wes and Pat have their horses outside and are waiting for you. What's your plan?" Bruce said.

"Bruce, it's time we took care of Owens and his men before they raid the cabins and burn them," Trent said.

"It sounds dangerous, Trent." Becky spoke up as she cleaned the pan her mother had used to wash Pony Boy's wound.

"Yup, it is," Trent said and waited for Becky to object to him going.

"Then you be careful," Becky said.

Trent nodded. "Well, I guess we better get going," he added before he turned and headed for the door.

"I didn't hear Becky complaining about you riding against Owens and his men," Wes said.

"Nope, she didn't object."

"Hmm, she's a lot tougher than when we left Boston," Wes said.

Pat poked Wes in the ribs with his elbow. "Yup, and so are you."

"Mount up, boys," Trent said as he climbed into the saddle.

"Wes, are you sure you want to join Pat and me?"

"Yeah, I'm real sure. I've wanted to collect the bounty on Owens for a while now."

"I thought you and Pat had your hearts set on joining a cattle drive," Trent said as they trotted their horses toward the canyons.

"I've come to understand that I don't like hard work. Shooting outlaws seems an easier way to make a living than punching cows," Wes said.

Trent nodded. "Yup, it is until you catch a bullet."

"Well, I reckon I'll try not to get shot."

"Me too," Pat said.

Trent shook his head. "Okay, but don't say I didn't warn you."

"Trent, what's the plan once we get to the canyon?" Pat asked.

"We'll wait until dark and then sneak in," Trent replied.

"Then what?" Wes asked.

"We kill them."

"All of them?"

"Yup, if'n they don't give themselves up."

"I guess Becky hasn't changed you as much as I thought she had."

The three fell silent as they rode through the woods. At the edge of the last pine thicket before the canyons, Trent held up his hand. "We stop here until just before dark. Then we ride on up into the canyons. Owens might have sentries posted to bushwhack us in case we tried to follow him. If so, he'll pull them back to the box canyon before dark. Owens don't realize we know the location of his hideout," Trent said as he dismounted. He walked over and leaned against one pine tree. "Wes, better get some rest," Trent called as Pat followed his example.

"How can y'all rest? We're fixing to get into a gunfight with a dozen outlaws."

"It's easy, Wes. Just lean back against a tree and close your eyes," Pat said.

"It ain't going to work for me. I'm as nervous as a hen with a fox sniffing around the chicken coop."

The sun hugged the horizon when Trent pulled his hat off the front of his face and sat up. Pat must have heard him because he too leaned forward. Trent nodded at Wes. The boy was asleep. "Wake him up and let's ride," Trent said as he stood.

Pat picked up a twig and tossed it onto Wes's chest.

Wes's eyes snapped open. "What?"

"You fell asleep," Pat said. "It's time to get moving."

"I wasn't asleep. I was just resting my eyelids," Wes said as he climbed to his feet."

Pat glanced at him and shook his head.

"Well, I was, I tell you," Wes said as he fetched his Quarter Horse.

"Make sure your pistol is loaded, Wes," Pat added as he mounted. "And also your Winchester. We'll use the long gun as much as possible."

"It is. I hope I have time to draw on this Owens fellow. I bet he thinks he's fast," Wes said.

"He might be," Trent said.

"I've been practicing every day. I'm much faster than I used to be," Wes bragged.

"Wes, it ain't going to come down to a duel in the street. Hopefully, we will use the rifles to pick them off one at a time until they give up," Trent said.

"Yeah, well, I've been practicing with a rifle too," Wes called out as he followed Trent and Pat out of the pines.

"No talking from here on," Trent ordered. "Owens's guards could still hide along the trail, thinking to ambush us. Of course, I doubt he thinks we can track him to the box canyon, so he might just have a guard posted on the rim. That's why we will leave our horses nearby and enter the canyon afoot."

"I hate walking," Wes complained.

"Stop your bellyaching. It ain't going to be a long walk," Pat said.

Wes didn't respond, and everyone fell silent. The light was fading when Trent called a halt and dismounted.

"We'll leave the horses here behind these rocks. The entrance to the canyon is just a little piece up the trail," Trent whispered. "And keep your eyes peeled for a sentry."

Wes nodded as he removed his rifle from its scabbard. He cradled it in his arm like Trent carried his Sharps. "Hmm, it's an uncomfortable position. I don't see how you can carry that heavy Sharps in the crook of your arm all the time," Wes whispered when Trent walked by him.

By the time they reached the path that led into the box canyon, the sun had disappeared and twilight had faded into darkness. Where the canyon walls narrowed, the sound of someone coughing froze the three men in their tracks.

Trent saw Pat draw his hunting knife and nodded. When Pat silently moved in the cough's direction, Trent placed his hand on Wes to hold him back until Pat dispatched the sentry. They didn't have to wait long. Trent heard a deep sigh and then a soft thud against the ground. He released his grip on Wes. They both continued along the path with Pat joining them a moment later. They soon emerged into the box canyon.

Owens had an enormous bonfire in front of the lean-to. Trent counted a dozen men sitting around the fire roasting pieces of meat on sticks poked into the fire. It reminded Trent of a bunch of young boys spending the night in the woods.

"What now?" Wes whispered as the sounds of loud voices and laughter reached them.

"Wes, you stay with me. Pat, make your way around to the other side of the lean-to. When you get in position, whistle like a whippoorwill. I'll fire the first shot. After that, shoot at will."

Pat disappeared into the dark.

"I got to learn to move like him," Wes whispered. He sighed. "Hmm, it looks like they're having fun cooking their supper. I wonder what they have at the end of their sticks. I bet it ain't possum meat."

"Ain't nothing wrong with possum. I like it," Trent replied in a low voice.

The sound of a whippoorwill drifted to their ears. "Pat's in position. Get ready. Aim at one man in the middle. I'll target one this side of the fire. We don't want to shoot the same man." Trent barely finished speaking when he fired his Sharps. The booming sound of the .50 caliber rifle echoed off the walls of the canyon. In quick succession, the crack of Wes's and Pat's Winchesters bounced off the walls.

Two outlaws slumped forward, one into the bonfire. The outlaw who caught Trent's bullet fell backward from the impact. The men around the bonfire froze for a moment. However, when the buffalo rifle boomed a second time and knocked an outlaw four feet backward, the men scattered.

They couldn't escape the sights of Pat's and Wes's Winchesters. The two men fired as fast as they could cock the lever action. Outlaws died when they squatted in the open to return fire. Others died running to the corral for their horses. The outlaws who jumped onto their bareback mounts met a .50 caliber bullet when they raced for the entrance.

The men who hadn't sought shelter in the lean-to died quickly. Those inside who watched their companions fall like flies shouted for surrender.

"Toss your guns out and then walk over and stand in front of the fire. If anyone opens fire from inside the lean-to, I'll kill everyone!" Trent shouted.

A moment later, two men walked out of the lean-to. One of them was Owens McGill.

"Wes, you stay here in case we missed one. Keep your rifle covering the lean-to," Trent said as he stepped forward. "If anyone opens fire from inside, kill Owens."

"Trent, I should have known it was you! Hell, I should have put you in the dirt the first time we met," Owens shouted.

"Yup, you could have tried. Then I would be in bed now and you up on boot hill."

Pat walked up to join Trent. He covered the three men with his pistols.

"Owens, if you have a man hiding in the lean-to, you best tell him to step outside. At the first shot, Wes will drill a hole through your head."

Owens didn't respond for a long moment. "Bart, toss your pistol out and follow it with your hands reaching for the sky," Owens ordered.

Nothing!

"I'll skin you alive, Bart, if you don't show yourself immediately!"

Someone tossed a pistol into the dirt. A moment later, a skinny man with a chaw of tobacco in his mouth stepped out from the lean-to. "I could have shot them both, Owens."

"They've got a rifle trained on me, Bart," Owens said.

"That's too bad," the man added as he walked up to the fire.

"Watch them, Pat. I'll search the lean-to," Trent said as he shifted his Sharps to the crook of his arm.

"It ain't natural for a fellow to carry a buffalo rifle all the time," Owens said when Trent walked into the lean-to.

"It didn't take long for Trent to spot the strongbox. Someone had already broken the padlock. Trent lifted the lid and took a step back. "Gold coins!" he mumbled.

"What did you say?" Pat asked.

Trent grabbed the handle of the strongbox and pulled it outside. "Gold coins, Pat. The box is full of gold!"

Pat rushed over and looked inside. "Now that's a sight for sore eyes!"

"You can have the gold if you'll let us go," Owens said.

Trent chuckled. "We already have it. And you."

"They'll hang us," the third man said. "And I just joined the gang. I ain't robbed nobody," he complained.

Pat shook his head. "Ride with a gang, hang with a gang. That's the golden rule, pardner."

"Wes, you can come in now," Trent yelled.

A moment later, Wes walked up to the campfire.

"He ain't even old enough to shave!" Owens swore.

"But old enough to kill a man," Wes said. "You want to draw on me, mister?"

Owens glanced over at Trent. "Is he serious?"

"Yup."

"Let's cut to the chase, Wes. Show him your quick draw," Pat said.

Suddenly, a pistol appeared in Wes's hand. He twirled it back into his holster. "Are you ready, mister?"

Owens shook his head. "I'll pass."

"Pat, I never get any fun," Wes complained.

"Hmm," Trent said. "You've been practicing, Wes."

"Yeah, every day, Trent. Every day."

"Pat, get some rope and tie them up," Trent said.

"Are we going to head back home now that we've captured our bounties?"

Trent shook his head. "No, I don't want any of these killers within a mile of Becky. We'll spend the night here, and tomorrow Wes and I will pack the dead outlaws across their horses and take Owens and his two amigos to Salt Flats."

"Shouldn't we go back to the cabin and get a wagon?" Pat asked.

"No, the horses will do. However, I want you to ride to the homestead and watch over things until Wes and I get back from Salt Flats.

"You mean I get to go with you this time, Trent?" Wes beamed.

"Yup."

"What about the gold coins?" Wes asked as he glanced into the strongbox.

"We turn it over to Sheriff Givens," Trent said.

"All of it?" Wes asked.

"Yup."

"Ah, shucks!" Wes said, sounding his age.

Chapter Fourteen
Sheriff Givens

The long column plodded across the prairie like a disjointed snake. Trent rode at the head of the column and Wes at the rear. Between them rode three live men and nine dead tied across their saddles.

To Wes's delight, Trent had allowed him to carry the strongbox of gold coins. Trent did it more to save Tex from having to carry the extra weight than to please Wes.

Trent kept his head on a swivel. He half-expected riders from McGregor's ranch to spot them and ride over to look. If that happened, he hoped the meeting wouldn't erupt into gunplay. However, except for cattle grazing slowly along the eastern horizon, nothing else moved across the short grass.

They reached the outskirts of Salt Flats without attracting unwanted attention. The sight of the nine bodies draped over horses had people scampering indoors to peek out the windows. Wagons pulled to the far side of the street to allow the procession to proceed solemnly through town.

Trent expected Sheriff Givens to emerge from the office, but he didn't. Trent tied Tex to the hitching post. "Wes, stay mounted and keep an eye on the live ones," he called over his shoulder as he took the steps to the porch.

Sheriff Givens paused in his conversation with a man sitting in front of his desk to glance up at Trent. The man in the chair had his back to Trent.

"What brings you back to Salt Flats? Collect that bounty on Owens McGill yet?" Sheriff Givens said and chuckled.

"Nope, I didn't. That's why I'm here. I've got nine dead men across their saddles and three in the saddle, one of which is Owens McGill."

Sheriff Givens's mouth dropped open. "You're poking fun at me, right, sodbuster?"

"Nope. Go out and have a look, Sheriff," Trent said.

"Boy, don't make me walk out there if you're not serious," Sheriff Givens said.

"Sheriff, you call me a boy again, and you ain't going to walk out the door," Trent said in a bitter tone that caused the man in the seat to turn around.

Cord McGregor!

"Howdy, Cord," Trent said, deliberately calling him by his first name. "I see you're back from Cheyenne. I hope you had no more stampedes."

McGregor sprung to his feet. "The half-breed!" he exclaimed.

Sheriff Givens glanced from one man to the other. "You two know one another?"

"Yup, Cord tried to stampede his cattle into the wagon train I traveled the Santa Fe Trail with, but it didn't work out so well for him."

McGregor pointed his finger at Trent. "Sheriff, he killed some of my cowhands! Arrest him!"

Sheriff Givens looked uncomfortable. "Mister McGregor, the Santa Fe Trail is out of my jurisdiction. If you had a beef against Trent, you should have taken it to the marshal in Wagon Mound."

"I'm taking my complaint to you now!" McGregor roared like a wounded bear.

Sheriff Givens shook his head. "Cord, my hands are tied."

"Well, mine aren't," McGregor said. "Trent, I'll hang you myself for gunning down my men."

"McGregor," Sheriff Givens said in a soft tone. "Let's not have any lynching talk in Salt Flats."

McGregor whipped around to face Sheriff Givens. "Sheriff, you best stay out of my way, or you'll get hurt," he said as he stormed over to the door. He jerked it open and froze when he saw the string of horses. "What's that, Sheriff?" McGregor shouted.

"That," Trent answered. "Is the entire Owens McGill gang. I brought them in for the bounty." Trent nodded at Sheriff Givens. "I also brought you the strongbox filled with gold coins they stole. I don't have any idea where they stole the gold from. Maybe you do, Sheriff?"

Sheriff Givens shoved Cord aside as he rushed onto the porch. "Why, that's the gold from the train robbery a while back." He glanced back at Trent as he stepped off the porch. "Where's the gold?"

"The young bounty hunter on the Quarter Horse is carrying the gold," Trent said.

"Sheriff," Owens said. "Trent and this boy and an Indian killed nine of my men in cold blood!"

Sheriff Givens glanced up at Owens. "Too bad he didn't shoot the rest of you. Would have saved me the trouble of hanging you."

Cord McGregor finally found his composure. "See, Sheriff, this half-breed is a killer. Arrest him!"

"Cord," Sheriff Givens said, "I have a wanted poster on Owens and his gang."

"No," Trent said. "I have it. But here, I don't need it anymore." Trent pulled the folded piece of paper out of his shirt pocket and handed it to the sheriff.

"Thanks, Trent. And I'll take the gold and put it in one of the jail cells for safekeeping."

"Wes, bring the sheriff the strongbox."

Wes slid off his horse and untied the strongbox. He struggled under its weight. He placed it on the edge of the porch and opened the lid.

"Cord, look at them gold coins. Ain't that a pretty sight?" Givens said.

McGregor shook his head. "Sheriff, I have more gold than that at my ranch house."

"You don't say," Sheriff Givens said, shaking his head.

"Sheriff," Wes said. "When do I get the bounty money?"

Sheriff Givens glanced at Trent. "The kid gets the money?"

Trent opened his mouth to answer.

"Sheriff," Wes said before Trent spoke. "They call me the Boston Kid. Remember that name. Someday I will be a famous bounty hunter."

"Well, Kid, if you had a part in capturing Owens, you are already famous," Sheriff Givens said.

"Y'all are talking like I ain't even here! It's making me mad," Owens said.

Sheriff Givens glanced up at the outlaw. "You're here now, but you ain't going to be around for long because you're a dead man walking."

"Cord." Trent nodded at the rancher. "Too bad the Apaches massacred the men you sent to burn me and my friend's cabins."

McGregor's face turned red. "You... you are the homesteader running sheep on my grazing range!" he declared. "Sheriff, arrest this sheepherder!"

Sheriff Givens shook his head. "Cord, you know there's no law against running sheep on one's own property. And that entire river valley near the canyons is government land open for settlers. And if you ask me, it's about time you recognized it!"

McGregor shook his head. "Givens, you'll be lucky to hold your job until the end of the week. You know you can't cross me and get away with it."

"Well, Cord, until that time comes, I plan on upholding the law. I'm sick and tired of you running roughshod over Salt Flats, and frankly, I think the mayor has had a bellyful of it too. So don't count your chickens before they hatch!"

"We'll see, Sheriff, we'll see," McGregor said as he stalked off the porch. He turned and hurried toward the saloon.

"Trent, you and the kid better git out of town. He's going to the saloon to get Red."

"I ain't afraid of this Red fellow, Trent," Wes said.

124 | RUSSELL J. ATWATER

"Yup, I know, but if I get you hurt in a gunfight, Becky would never marry me, Wes. So do me a favor and let's ride out of town."

"I'm doing it for you, Trent, and not because I'm afraid of Red." Wes walked back and vaulted onto his horse. "Sheriff, have that bounty money ready for me when I return."

"Okay, Kid, I will, but get out of here now. I don't want a gunfight in the middle of town."

Trent kicked his heels lightly into Tex's sides. The big palomino only took two steps to reach a full gallop. Wes's Quarter Horse took even less distance. Trent didn't pull up until they were a mile out of town.

"Trent, I don't like running away from a fight," Wes said as they slowed their horses to a walk.

"Neither do I, Wes, but we have to think of your family. What will happen to them if we get killed in a shootout with Red and his buddies? Pat will take care of Red when the time comes. I've just been putting it off."

"Why? Are you afraid that Pat might not be fast enough on the draw?" Wes asked.

"Not so much that as what happens if Pat kills Red. Now that I realize that Sheriff Givens is trying to do the right thing, I'm okay with a gunfight between the two. I just didn't want Pat to win and then get hanged for killing a white man."

"Do you think McGregor will replace Givens as sheriff with someone who will do his bidding without questioning if it legal or not?"

"I don't know, Wes. I sort of got the notion the town of Salt Flats has had enough of Cord McGregor," Trent said.

"Are you fast enough to outdraw Red?"

"No, he's faster than me," Trent answered without hesitation. "I don't pretend to be a quick draw artist. Pat's the gunslinger. I'm the sharpshooter."

"Do you think I could beat Red to the draw?" Wes asked, his voice a little hesitant.

"Before I saw you draw your pistol back at the box canyon, I would have said no. However, since I've seen how much you've improved, I'm not sure. Maybe."

"Do you think I'm as fast as Pat on the draw now, Trent?"

"That's a hard one to answer, Wes. You shook me with your hand speed. With Pat, it's not so much hand speed as it is technique and sure willpower. He's one of a kind. He's one with his pistols."

"You make Pat sound strange."

"He is, a little," Trent admitted.

"But, Trent, you're also strange. You carry your buffalo rifle in the crook of your arm everywhere you go. Like Owens said back at the box canyon, it ain't natural."

"I reckon not, but without my Sharps, I would have ended up on boot hill a long time ago," Trent said.

"Are you ever going to put it down for good?"

"Yup, the day I marry your sister."

Chapter Fifteen
Cattlemen vs Sheepmen

"Trent, I want to keep the sheep closer to the cabin after what you told me about your meeting with Cord McGregor. I fear he'll send another party of men to kill or drive off my sheep," Bruce said as both men sat in chairs in front of the Cowans' cabin.

Trent nodded. "Yup, I agree. It's only been two weeks since Wes and I visited Salt Flats. So far, we haven't seen a sign of McGregor's men. But I don't think he'll let you keep running sheep in the river valley."

"Neither do I. I just don't want Lois and Becky to get hurt," Bruce said.

"I ain't going to let anything happen to either of them," Trent blurted.

"Yeah, I know, Trent, I know," Bruce said with a faint smile. "Ah, Wes is chomping at the bit to get back to Salt Flats to collect the reward money on Owens McGill and his men. I'm afraid to see him return to Salt Flats. I'm sure he'll run into gunplay. I think he wants to have a duel with this Red fellow to prove to everyone he's a gunslinger and not a boy anymore."

"Where are Pat and Wes?" Trent asked.

"Where do you think? Down in the river. Sometimes it's easy to forget how young they both are until you see them splashing in the river like two kids."

"I'm glad Pat is enjoying himself. He didn't have much of a childhood. Pat's been wearing a gun belt forever, it seems. He had to since my father traveled through rough country to reach all the little trading outposts. My father made me carry a rifle for the same reason. The Apaches killed our parents when Pat was fourteen. He's been stoic ever since. Wes is the first person he's made friends with since our parents died."

At the first sound of horse hooves pounding against the ground, Trent sprung out of his chair and lifted the Sharps to his shoulder. The moment the rider appeared with a bandana covering his face, Trent fired. The bullet knocked the man off the back of his horse. As more masked riders emerged from the woods, Trent shoved Bruce toward the door as he drew his pistol.

Trent cringed as he heard Becky scream. He shut out her and her mother's screams as he shot the next rider in the chest. Then as five riders abreast charged out of the woods, he fanned his hammer, hitting all five men. But a horde of mounted men followed those.

Trent grabbed his rifle and ran for the door as bullets sprayed the surrounding ground. Bruce slammed the door behind Trent before poking his shotgun out the window and firing. His blast knocked a man out of the saddle.

By that time, Trent had reloaded his pistol. He ran to the window, and seemingly not taking aim, fired six shots in rapid succession. Six riders, passing by the window, hit the dirt.

As Trent reloaded his pistol, he heard gunshots from the direction of the flock. He knew Pony Boy had opened fire. He just hoped he wouldn't catch a bullet as he heard the attackers returning pistol fire.

"Where's Pat and Wes? We need them," Bruce shouted as the mounted men circled the cabin and fired through the windows.

Suddenly, the sound of rapidly firing pistols echoed off the cabin. Trent, who had glanced out the window to return fire, saw riders falling off their horses right and left. In a matter of seconds, over half the horses ran riderless. Trent fired at the remaining mounted men, hitting four before he emptied his Colt. The rest of the men fled like scalded dogs.

Trent pulled back from the window. He glanced back at Becky, huddled in the corner. "It's over. They're gone!"

"Dang McGregor!" Bruce shouted.

"I've got to see about Pony Boy!" Trent said as he rushed out the door. Trent didn't stop running until he reached the flock. He noticed several dead sheep. "Pony Boy!" Trent shouted.

Lobo and Pup ran up to Trent.

Pony Boy popped up from behind a huge blueberry bush. He pointed over at the riderless horses. "Pony Boy kills palefaces!" he shouted.

Trent breathed a sigh of relief as he patted Pup on her head while Lobo laid down and exposed his belly in a sign of submission. Pup had had a litter of six puppies under the wagon. One puppy looked exactly like Lobo.

Trent heard horses. He whipped around and lifted his rifle to his shoulder, only to immediately lower it.

"Is everyone okay?" Wes called out.

"Yup," Trent replied.

"We killed a slew of them," Wes added.

"What do we do with the bodies?" Pat asked.

"We load them on the wagon and haul them to McGregor's ranch," Trent said.

"This time I'm going," Wes declared in a determined tone.

"Yup, and so is Pony Boy. We need everyone in case there's gunplay at the end of the trip." Trent said.

"I hope there's gunplay," Wes said. "I'm itching to face this Red fellow. I want to see if he is as fast as everyone makes him out to be."

"Don't be so eager to get yourself killed," Trent said as he turned to head back to the cabin. "Pony Boy, leave Lobo and Pup with the sheep and come with me."

"Wes, don't be so quick to die," Pat said.

"I'm faster than that darn cowboy," Wes said as he and Pat rode alongside Trent and Pony Boy.

Trent shook his head. "How do you know, Wes? You've never seen Red draw his pistol."

"I just know how fast the Boston Kid is with an iron," Wes replied.

Trent glanced up at Pat. "You created him. He's your responsibility."

Bruce hurried out to meet them. "Are the sheep all right?"

"Several of them are dead. After we leave, you can take Becky and Miss Lois out and butcher them. I guess we can smoke the meat," Trent said as he walked past Bruce toward the wagon.

Bruce stopped and watched Trent. "Where are you taking the wagon?"

"I'm returning Cord McGregor's men to the ranch," Trent said. He nodded over at Pat. "You and Wes fetch the team. I'll get the harnesses ready," Trent added.

"You should just drag them off in the woods and leave them. I don't want you getting in a gunfight returning the bodies to McGregor," Becky said.

"Becky, it's the right thing to do," Trent said.

"The right thing, Trent Mcleod, is for you not to get hurt," Becky replied with her hands on her hips.

Wes walked by Trent, leading one of the Morgan mares. "Hogtied, and she will wear the britches," he leaned over to whisper.

It didn't take them long to hitch the two mares to the wagon. Once they finished, Pat drove the wagon over to the nearest body.

"Leave the bandanas on their faces," Trent said. "I'm thinking of taking the bodies to Salt Flats to show Sheriff Givens. Let him remove their bandanas and identify them as Cord's men."

"That's a good idea. Let the sheriff deal with McGregor," Pat called out from the seat of the wagon. "It might save us a gunfight. Miss Becky will be pleased with that!"

"I'm all for stopping the killing," Trent said as he grabbed the boots of one of the dead men while Wes took his shoulder. They placed the corpse on the floor of the wagon.

"How many men does McGregor have to lose? We have done nothing to him!" Becky said.

"The sheep threaten his way of life, or so he thinks," Trent said.

"Becky," Lois called. "Come and help with the pans and knives. We might as well butcher the dead sheep."

After they had loaded the last of the dead, Trent took a moment to walk over to where Becky and Lois worked, butchering the sheep.

"Becky, I have an important question to ask," Trent said.

Becky straightened up from working on the carcass and wiped her forehead with the back of her bloody hand. "Yeah, what?"

Trent hesitated.

"What? I'm right in the middle of removing this liver. Speak up!"

Trent cleared his throat. "Will you marry me?" he exclaimed.

A stunned look flashed across Becky's face. She glanced over at her mother. Lois put the back of her hand over her mouth as she cried out in joy.

"Trent McLeod, you dare ask me to marry you when I'm up to my elbows inside a sheep!"

"Yup! It seemed like the perfect time. We will be a pioneering family, and butchering sheep will be a big part of our lives," Trent replied.

"Yes, you big galoot, I'll marry you."

Trent stepped forward to give Becky a quick peck on the lips. "Much more after we are married," Trent said as he turned and skipped back to the wagon.

Wes shook his head. "You are a lost soul now, Trent. Yep, a lost soul."

"But a happy one," Trent said as he beamed a smile from ear to ear.

Wes shook his head as he slapped the reins against the backs of the mares, "Giddyup." Neither one spoke until the wagon pulled up to the cabin. "Pa, Trent asked Becky to marry him!" Wes shouted.

Bruce took his hat off and slapped it against his britches. "Well, doggone it, it's about time!"

Trent blushed.

"Son, that's the best news I've heard in an age!" Bruce said with a big smile.

Trent's face turned redder as Pat glanced at him from atop Leo. Pat just nodded.

"Okay, let's get the wagon rolling, Wes," Trent said.

"Trent, don't get yourself killed before you marry my daughter," Bruce yelled as the wagon moved.

"I'll take care of him, Pa," Wes yelled back.

"And who will take care of you, Wes?" Pat called from his horse.

"I watch Wes," Pony Boy said.

Wes shook his head. "Hmm, I'm in trouble!"

No one spoke until they turned onto the prairie road.

"I wonder if Chief Red Hawk and his tribe outran the cavalry?" Wes asked.

"I'm sure they did," Pat answered. He rode beside Wes. "They know the land better than the troopers. And if the soldiers get too close, he'll set up a series of traps to slow them down. After facing a few ambushes, the captain will turn back to the fort."

"I hope you're right, Pat," Wes said.

Pat and Pony Boy had to urge cattle out of the way as Wes drove the wagon through a large herd.

"Where are all the drovers?" Wes asked.

Trent tilted his head back. "In the wagon bed."

"I bet he ain't going to convince any more of his ranch hands to raid Pa's sheep," Wes said.

"He don't have to. He can hire new men who live by their guns instead of punching cows. You forget that Cord McGregor is a rich man, Wes," Trent replied.

Wes shook his head. "Yeah, it's just hard for me to come to grips with the fact that a rancher can be so rich."

"Texas has lots of rich ranchers," Pat called out.

"They run the state of Texas," Trent said.

Wes suddenly got a glowing look. "Hey, I wonder if Sheriff Givens will have our reward money," Wes said.

"He better have it," Pat said.

"Maybe he's no longer sheriff?" Trent said.

"Then whoever took his place better have it," Wes added.

"We'll soon find out." Trent nodded. "I see the building ahead."

"It looks like we made it without running into any of McGregor's men," Wes said.

"Wes, if there's trouble, let's not be the ones who start it," Trent cautioned.

"Dang it, Trent, you just don't want me to have any fun," Wes said.

"Killing people ain't my idea of having fun!" Trent said in a scolding tone.

Wes shrugged.

Few people were about the dusty main street. The ones outside scurried about as though frightened.

Pat motioned toward the hitching posts in front of the saloon. "Looks as though the saloon is busting at the seams."

"Most of the horses have McGregor's brand," Trent said as Wes rode past.

"Looks like I ain't going to look far for trouble," Wes said.

"Pull over to the sheriff's office," Trent said. When Wes stopped the team of Morgan mares, Trent leaped down from the wagon. "Everyone, wait here. And don't stray." Not knowing who he would find behind the desk, Trent opened the door.

Sheriff Givens removed his boots from the top of his desk and put down the newspaper. He shook his head. "Trent, I was praying I wouldn't see you today."

"You expected me, Sheriff?"

"Yup, when I saw only half of McGregor's men who rode out of town this morning return, I suspected they paid your homestead a visit. I guess you brought a wagon, and I'm afraid to ask what it contains."

"The other half of McGregor's men," Trent replied. "I'm only guessing since they all are wearing bandanas over their lower faces. You can see for yourself, Sheriff. We were attacked by masked men and defended ourselves."

Sheriff Givens shook his head. I feared this would happen. I warned McGregor he wasn't above the law."

"Actually, I'm surprised to see you're still the sheriff in Salt Flats. I figured from the way Cord talked the last time I was in town, he would have your star pinned on someone else's chest."

Sheriff Givens shrugged. "It wasn't from his lack of trying. However, the mayor wouldn't go along with Cord's request. He's stuck with me, and Cord's not very happy."

"Sheriff, I have to ask you, do you have the reward money for Owens?" Trent looked at the empty jail cells behind the sheriff's desk. "Where is Owens? Have you already hanged him?"

"I sent him up to Dumas. I think the judge sentenced him to hang on Saturday. I've got the bounty money in a carpetbag under the bunk in the first cell."

"Bring it out when you come. Wes will want to see it," Trent said as he turned to leave.

"Does he have the money?" Wes asked the moment Trent stepped onto the porch.

"Yup, he's bringing it."

A moment later, Sheriff Givens walked out the door with the money wrapped in a brown paper bag. "I've got your money, boys," Sheriff Givens called out. Who do I give it to?"

Pat nodded at Wes. "Give it to the Boston Kid, the famous bounty hunter," Pat said with a stoic expression.

Trent, however, broke into laughter.

"Have your fun, Trent, but someday it'll be true," Wes said.

Trent nodded. "Yup, I'm sure it will be." He waited until the sheriff handed the money to Wes before he added. "Sheriff, have a look at these outlaws and see if you recognize any of them."

Sheriff Givens shook his head as he followed Trent to the rear of the wagon. "My word, what a waste of lives," Sheriff Givens said.

Trent reached down and pulled the bandanna down on one of the dead men's faces. "Do you recognize him?"

"Yeah, that Roger Littlefinger, one of Cord's ranch hands. He gets drunk, and I'm always locking him up overnight. I guess he's seen his last drink." Sheriff Givens glanced toward the saloon when he heard voices. "Yonder comes trouble!" he added, nodding toward the group of men walking toward the wagon.

Chapter Sixteen
The Showdown

"That's Red in the lead," Sheriff Givens said. He turned from the wagon and took two steps toward the approaching men. "What can I do for you, boys?"

"What's in the wagon, Sheriff?" Red demanded.

"Some dead masked outlaws that attacked these homesteaders."

"Move aside, Sheriff. I want to look-see," Red ordered.

"Yeah, maybe you'll recognize some of them," Sheriff Givens said as he took a step to the right. "Be my guest, have a look."

Red stalked up and stuck his head inside the covered wagon. "Rog!" Red declared. "They killed Rog, Sheriff, arrest them!" Red glanced behind him. "Johnny, ride to the ranch and get Mister McGregor and don't take all day." Red turned back to the sheriff. "Well, ain't you going to arrest them?"

Sheriff Givens shook his head. "Nope. If Rog still sucked air, I would arrest him and the others. I don't cotton to running settlers off their homesteads."

"Mister McGregor will put you in the dirt, Sheriff, along with these settlers."

Wes jumped down from the wagon. "Fella, I heard about as much as I can take of your flapping lips. You need to shut your trap."

Red turned to face Wes. "Boy, get back on your wagon before I take you over my knee and give you a spanking."

The men behind Red roared in laughter.

Trent shook his head. "Red, Wes doesn't like to be called boy."

"I don't give a fart in the wind what the boy likes or dislikes," Red replied.

Wes moved away from Trent and the wagon. "Mister Red, I'm calling you out!"

"Now, wait a minute!" Sheriff Givens said. "He ain't old enough to shave, Trent. You've got to stop this nonsense."

Trent glance over at Pat.

His brother shrugged. "You got to let him do it."

Trent nodded. "Yup, I guess we do at that."

"This is pure murder! Red is a gunslinger with a reputation as long as my arm," Sheriff Givens said. "Trent, you got to stop this!"

"Sheriff," Red called out. "Just step aside and let me send the boy to boot hill, and then I'll send his friends to keep him company," Red said.

Sheriff Givens raised his hands in surrender. "I give up. I'm wasting my breath. Fly to it, boys!"

"Boy, you are not the first greenhorn I've put in the dirt, just the youngest," Red said as they both moved over in the middle of the street.

"I wish I could say that you are the first man I've killed, mister, but you aren't. However, you might be the quickest on the draw, but I won't know that until I shoot you."

Red glanced over at his friends. "You hear that, boys, the kid thinks he's faster than I am."

Several men from the group laughed.

"Red," one of them said, "these settlers have sent a lot of our friends to boot hill. They didn't do that, being slow on the draw."

"Shut up, Jack. I ain't asking you for your opinion."

"Mister Red, are you trying to give me a sun burn standing out in the sun?"

"Boy, that mouth of yours just got you killed!" Red said. "Go for your iron whenever you're ready."

Wes shook his head. "Nope, the Boston Kid doesn't draw first."

"Boston Kid!" Red said as though he couldn't believe his ears. "Fellas, did you hear that? The kid is calling himself the Boston Kid. Red laughed. "Okay, Kid, I'll put it on your grave marker. Now draw!"

"Nope, you first, Red. Or do you want to stand here all day?"

Red glanced over at Sheriff Givens. "Okay, Sheriff, you see it. The kid is forcing me to draw first."

Sheriff Givens didn't respond.

Red shrugged. He took a deep breath. When he let the air out, he reached for his Colt. He had lifted his pistol a couple of inches from his holster when the crack of a pistol sounded. Red's gun slipped from his fingers as a look of shock spread quickly across his freckled face. He glanced down at the hole in the breast of his shirt before he crumpled to the ground.

"Dang it, I thought he would take all day to reach for his pistol," Wes said as he twirled his Colt back into his holster.

Sheriff Givens shook his head. "Now I've seen it all!" he declared.

The group of men from the saloon stared at their fallen friend in silence as the sound of horses galloping down the street caught their attention.

"It's Cord McGregor and his sons," Sheriff Givens announced.

Trent stepped up beside Sheriff Givens. "I know Gary and Jeremiah. Who are the other two sons?"

"Wally and Major, and the sixth man is the foreman, Clint," Sheriff Givens said.

Trent nodded. "Yup, I've met Clint."

Cord McGregor's face looked stony enough to freeze water as he pulled his horse to a stop at the back of the wagon. He glanced over at Red lying in the middle of the street. "Which one of the half-breeds killed Red?"

Sheriff Givens nodded toward Wes. "Neither, it was the boy."

"That's not possible. Red was fast as lightning! You can't tell me that greenhorn boy gunned down Red, Sheriff. Hell, he ain't even old enough to shave."

Sheriff Givens shrugged. "It's a fact, take it or leave it. I saw it start to finish."

"Red was kind of slow on the draw, Mister McGregor," Wes said. "I need more practice. Have you got anyone quicker?"

Cord McGregor glanced at Sheriff Givens.

The sheriff shrugged.

"What's in the wagon?" Cord asked.

"The men you sent to burn our homesteads and drive off our sheep… well, half of them," Trent said, "He pointed over at the men from the bar. "I suspect that's the other half."

"Gary, look in the wagon," Cord ordered.

Gary slid out of the saddle and walked over and glanced into the bed of the wagon. He backpedaled. "Daddy, it's Rog and over a dozen of our men. They're all dead."

"Sheriff Givens, arrest these half-breeds. They murdered my men," Cord shouted. "Or else I'll shoot them where they stand!"

Wes nodded toward where Red lay in the middle of the street. "Mister McGregor, that approach didn't work out for Red or your men. We ain't the sodbusters you're used to pushing around. You must be plain dumb not to have noticed that by now."

When Wes said the word dumb, Jeremiah reached for his gun. Pat shot him in his gun hand before he pulled the pistol out of his holster.

Pony Boy had drawn his pistol but hadn't fired. "Hmm, Pony Boy no get to shoot paleface."

"Daddy! I'm hit!" Jeremiah shouted as he grabbed his right hand.

"Put your pistol away, Pony Boy," Pat said as he twirled his right pistol back into his holster. "The next man who reaches for his iron is dead," he added.

"Cord, the only way you and your sons are riding away is if you swear to leave us be on our homestead in front of these men and the sheriff," Pat said. "If you aren't going to pledge to stop harassing the Cowans and Trent, then go for your irons. I've had a bellyful of your tyranny. And if you turn to ride away, Wes and I'll shoot you in the back even if it makes us wanted men!"

"Sheriff, you heard them threaten me. Arrest them," Cord said as he pointed his finger at Pat.

Sheriff Givens shook his head. "Cord, they have broken no laws."

"They killed my men!" McGregor shouted.

"They defended their land. You have a right to defend yourself in Texas, Cord. No, if I will arrest someone, it would be you."

"Swear, Cord, or you and your sons die on the spot. Because there ain't no way under the sun that you six men will stand if you draw on Wes and me."

"Sheriff," McGregor's voice took on a pleading tone.

"Pa, we can outdraw them. It's five against two," Gary said.

"Shut up, you fool. Didn't you see how fast he drew his pistol? And dang it, the kid outdrew Red."

Gary dropped his head.

"Mister McGregor," Clint said. "It's time to let your beef with these men run its course."

"But dang it, they're running sheep!" Cord said

"On their own land," Clint replied. "Trent, do you promise to keep your sheep on your property and not graze them on the open range?"

"Yes, I do, Clint," Trent said immediately.

Sheriff Givens nodded at Cord McGregor. "Is it a deal, Cord?"

McGregor didn't answer for a long moment. "Yeah, it's a deal. But the moment they graze their sheep on public land, I'll send my men to burn their homesteads."

"I will keep my part of the agreement, but Cord, what makes you think your men would have any better success the next time? And let me tell you if there is a next time, I'll sit back so far away that you can't see me and pick you and your sons off with my buffalo rifle one at a time," Trent said as he shifted the Sharps in the crook of his arm.

Without another word, Cord McGregor whipped his horse around and spurred it savagely. The horse lurched forward in shock.

"I should shoot him for the way he treats that horse," Trent said.

"Okay," Sheriff Givens shouted at the men from the saloon. "The entertainment is over. Two you grab Red and put him in the wagon." After the men left, Sheriff Givens nodded his head at Pat. "Son, would you have shot them in the back?"

Pat nodded. "Yup."

"Well, I'm just glad it didn't come down to that," Sheriff Givens said.

"So am I, Sheriff," Pat said. "Wes, hop back up into the wagon and let's get these men over to the undertaker."

After they finished unloading the bodies at the undertaker, Wes turned the wagon south.

"Pony Boy, ride in the wagon," Trent said. "I need to borrow your horse. I've got to visit Preacher Jetson and set the wedding date."

"Uh, shouldn't you discuss that with Sis?" Wes asked.

"Nope, I'm not as hogtied as you might think, Wes," Trent said as he mounted Pony Boy's horse. "I'll catch up with you all."

Epilogue

Trent kissed Becky after he climbed into the seat of the wagon.

"You're married now, so I can't complain about you kissing my daughter," Bruce called from the back of the wagon.

"You could, but it wouldn't do you any good," Trent said as he kissed her a second time before slapping the reins against the backs of the two mares.

Becky glanced at Preacher Jetson as he stood in the door of the adobe building. "Thank you! It was a beautiful ceremony," she said as Trent turned the wagon around.

"It was my first wedding," Preacher Jetson called back. "Now I can go to the saloon and have a drink."

"Trent, I just wish Pat and Wes had stayed for the wedding," Becky said. "I miss them both."

"Those two boys have sand in their boots. They didn't want any part of Trent getting hitched," Bruce said, answering for Trent.

"I just hope they don't take up bounty hunting," Becky said.

"I'm afraid that's exactly what they will do," Trent said.

"Trent," Lois said. "I still haven't gotten used to seeing you without the rifle in the crook of your arm."

"Well, Miss Lois, I ain't a frontiersman anymore. I'm a family man now... or hope to be soon.

"Pa, do you think Mister McGregor will keep the peace?" Becky asked.

"He has so far. I hope it lasts. Trent and I have kept our sheep on the homesteads. We've lived up to our side of the bargain," Bruce said.

The two couples fell silent as they enjoyed the company of their partner. Trent spotted cowboys herding cattle, but the sight didn't alarm him like it would have a month ago before the showdown in Salt Flats.

He was still amazed Wes had outdrawn Red. Deep in his heart, he had thought Wes would die that day. The speed of Wes's draw had surprised him, and he suspected it had Pat too. The boy from Boston had undoubtedly grown into a man. He felt sorry for any outlaws who faced off against Wes and Pat.

"Look," Becky said, breaking into Trent's thoughts. "Isn't that an Apache in the pines near the river?"

Trent automatically reached for his Sharps, only to realize he had left it at the cabin. Instead, he touched his fingers to his Colt and watched the man urge his horse toward them at a trot.

"Is he friendly?" Bruce said as he grabbed his scattergun.

Trent hesitated as he squinted at the mounted figure. "It's Chief

Red Hawk," Trent finally declared.

"What's he doing back?" Bruce asked.

Trent shrugged. "I guess we're fixing to find out. I just wish Pat were here. He's much better at sign language then I am."

As Chief Red Hawk neared the wagon, he held up his hand in the sign of peace. For the next several minutes, Trent traded signs with the chief. When the chief finally turned his horse around and rode back into the pines, Trent faced Bruce and Lois.

"The Apaches got away from the army and returned to their valley. Chief Red Hawk has reconsidered and wants peace," Trent said.

Bruce shook his head. "It might last for a while, but I don't see Cord McGregor sharing his grazing land with Apaches. With the buffalo gone, it's only going to be a matter of time before some of his men butcher a few of Cord's cattle."

"Yup, but the Apaches do some farming. Hopefully, they'll be able to feed themselves with farming and hunting. If they kill Cord's cows, well, it ain't going to go well for them."

"Whatever happens, we must keep out of any confrontation between the Apaches and Cord," Becky said.

"Nope, I will give a quarter of my flock to Chief Red Hawk," Bruce proclaimed. "And I will send Pony Boy to teach them how to care for the sheep in exchange for a wife for him."

Trent smiled. "That might solve the problem. But Chief Red Hawk will have to keep his sheep off Cord's grazing land," Trent said.

"Yeah, Trent... you must explain that to him. If he expands his flock before long, the sheep will supplement his people with a continuous supply of meat and wool," Bruce said.

"And Pony Boy will get a wife!" Lois proclaimed.

The End

Thanks for taking the time to read this story. A positive review on Amazon would be appreciated.

Made in the USA
Coppell, TX
10 March 2021

51518285R10088